BORN ON THE EDGE

A Folly Beach Mystery

MICHELE NUTWELL

Born on the Edge

A Folly Beach Mystery

2011

PROLOGUE

In the darkness the howling started, a staccato of high pitched shrieks alarming in both sound and consistency. Begging, almost humanly so, to be terminated in whatever fashion would be most expeditious. Happy to be of service, a matted grayish black creature sailed through the air and pounced, silencing the objectionable fracas. The victor remained perched, belly-rumbling chatter daring the noises to restart.

"Damn cat, I heard it, nothing wrong with my hearing, you know that by now." The woman sat up in bed and reached towards the lamp, somewhere there next to the furry beast atop the alarm clock. A twist of somewhat shaky fingers produced a soft glow of light, which in turn made visible the items on the bedside table. Aforementioned cat on alarm clock, water dripping out of a glass knocked over by said cat, eyeglasses, notepad and pen, a variety of small medicine bottles.

Unfolding the glasses and perching them on her nose, the woman squinted at the clock. Three a.m. and all is well, she thought, lifting the cat off. He sat motionless as she unsuccessfully combed through his tangled hair with crooked fingers and listened while she mused aloud.

"Theodora is coming tonight, I can feel it. The others have left their tracks and tonight is her turn, she only comes when the moon is full. She's the smartest of them all, yes she is," the woman told the cat.

"By the light of the silvery moon," she warbled, turning sideways in bed. Her practiced hands, yes, crooked and shaky but by damn, she could do this, took hold of the prosthetic device by the table and expertly attached it to the stub of her left leg. She firmly planted it along her right leg and arose, sending the cat sacrificially to the floor.

Although her gait was stilted, she went through her routine quickly. Black coffee, a splash of water on her face, quick brush of the teeth. She put the glasses back on, meeting her reflection in the mirror almost shyly. The thick lenses magnified her fading eyes. She didn't mind that the color was washing away, like water diluting a good brandy, but there was no denying her sight was fading.

"Damn diabetes," she muttered, not complaining, because she didn't do that, just stating the facts. Well, she'd been watching over Theodora for many years now, and the loss of one leg and a little foggy vision certainly wasn't changing that.

She gathered the things she needed for her foray into the darkness, starting with her hand-carved teak cane. Her house keys went in her jacket pocket and the flashlight fit snugly in her right hand. All she needed now was the dog.

He stood like a sentinel by the front door, or maybe like one of those funny guards over in London who never blink, she thought. He regarded her with solemn blue eyes, waiting for the command which would free him in to the night. She'd picked him out at the local pet shelter, choosing him right away out of all the others.

He smiled at her now, showing outlandishly long teeth. She'd named him Tusk.

Flashlight in one hand, cane in the other, no need for a leash as Tusk was voice trained, they ventured off. Across the street to the walkover that deposited the two on the beach, which was where it got a bit tricky, but the site was close by.

The moon hid her face nervously in the clouds, but a full moon it was, darting from one dark cloud to another. The flashlight illuminated the coarse sand like a beacon the two followed until they reached the tracks.

"Tusk, sit," the woman commanded. She bent down and gently brushed the sand, sifting until she felt the ping-pong like eggs.

"Theodora, you old biddy, you did it again. Close to 100 babies, I'd say. Now let's try to keep folks away."

She slowly made a square around the nesting site, using the orange police style tape she'd left yesterday. Her thoughts went again to Theodora, the female loggerhead turtle who'd come back every year for almost twenty years to this exact spot to lay her eggs. The woman felt her eyes misting up, wondering how many more years she, or Theodora for that matter, had left.

"Ah, well, Thea, we've had a good run, no matter......," she stopped talking and listened, to something, someone other than the waves and seagulls.

A voice; a man's voice, she thought, not happy sounding. Who in the world was out here at this time? She strained to hear, caught words and then a strange popping sound. Her eyes widened, Tusk growled.

Around the corner of the nearby sand dune a figure whipped to life and stumbled over the carefully placed orange tape, spewing curses as the woman tried to back up. Tusk lunged, a streak in the air cut short by an awful, sudden pop and the woman opened her mouth to say "No!", not quite making it as some hard piece of metal crashed against her skull.

And just as swiftly the peacefulness of the ocean returned, muffled waves breaking on the shore as quietly as possible. The full moon now seemed bent to hide, as if chased, behind every available cloud. Even the wind fled, whimpering across the sea so the stillness was complete.

Then somewhere, in the darkness, a howling began, plaintively at first, continuing to rise as it went unanswered until it reached a crescendo echoing the Atlantic.

CHAPTER ONE

The blare of the alarm zapped me awake, and for once I didn't mind. In fact, I might not sleep for a couple weeks or so. Anything to get the dratted dream director to leave me be. He first began appearing in my previously almost dreamless nights right around the time I was finding dead bodies, surfers to be precise. But that's another story.

I silenced the noise with a quick smack, catching a few long black hairs off my cat in the process. Sampson hissed. Well, he shouldn't be sleeping on my bedside table. Apparently he agreed with me, and relocated himself to my lap as I reached for my glasses and squinted at the time. Yep, here I was once again awake at the ungodly hour of 4:30 am., just so I could subject my body to an early morning run, penance for the beer and wings I'd consumed yesterday. Hey, what are you supposed to partake in while watching the first football games of the season?

So here it was, bright and early on a Monday morning, and in order to exercise I had to get my rear end in gear before my first appointment of the day. My name is Kell Palevac and I work for *The Archipelago,* a newspaper covering Charleston, South Carolina. My job is to report on happenings in the city of Folly Beach, an eclectic little beach town I am happy to call home. My town is never boring, hence neither is my job. Until a few months ago it was a fairly peaceful situation for me on Folly. Before the dead bodies which introduced the director of my dreams, who didn't seem to want to take a bow.

I huddled with my cat under the warm covers, tugging them a bit. Nothing happened, because my covers were pulled tightly by the rather large body stretched out next to me in my queen sized bed. I yanked a bit harder.

"Geeze, Fred, this has gone on long enough, don't you think?" Really, he had his own bed, and was milking this whole dead body thing just a bit too long. At first I had appreciated his company. I was slowly getting over my nightmares now, well, except for last night, and it was simply time for Fred to sleep alone.

He didn't answer, but his legs started moving in his sleep, which practically sent Sampson and me over the edge of the bed.

"Hey, quit with the chasing cats in your sleep routine, you're pushing me," I said to my rather large Great Dane. "And wake up. You're coming for a run."

Fred's legs stopped abruptly, so I knew he had heard and was now determined to remain as still as possible. Sampson was deposited on to the hardwood floors as I finally crawled out and sleep-walked my way in search of coffee. I'd gotten pretty good at setting the coffee maker the night before these early morning outings, so all I had to do was grab a cup, toss in the sugar and cream, and wait for the caffeine to work its magic. While my brain responded I did my habitual attempts to greet the morning, putting my contacts in, hooking my cell phone to my running shorts and tying my shoes. Grabbing Fred's leash, I took a deep breath.

He was now spread out so he occupied both sides of the bed, with Sampson curled up in the little corner left over near the pillows.

"Fred. Get up. I mean it."

He rolled over on to his back with his legs sticking up in the air, eyes closed.

"Forget it, fur face, the dead dog routine's not working today. Up!" I tried to make my voice come out as serious as possible, but at this early hour I sounded like a tired frog.

I hooked Fred's leash to his collar and pulled. Nothing happened so I pulled a little harder and my feet slid out from under me and I crashed on my butt. Fred stood up and growled, leaping to the floor where I sat, licking my face.

"Thanks, buddy, I'm okay. Do not sit down!"

I got up, yanking Fred along with me as I located a flashlight and the pepper spray the police had given me after my last escapade. I had asked for a gun, but I'm probably not getting one.

Closing my front door behind us, I put my keys in their hiding place under the potted hibiscus plant. I'd added some creeping jenny, and the bright green leaves were trailing quite nicely over the edges of the pot. I have no idea where I got my green thumb. Not from my mom, she forgets to water. She is an excellent cook, while

I, however, can barely boil eggs. This made me remember I was out of eggs. Out of milk, bread, you name it. Time to call Mazo's Market for a food delivery. I made a mental note to do so as Fred and I made our way across the street to the beach.

I decided to head to the right, not eagerly anticipating my two mile course up to the Holiday Inn and back. Four miles would certainly offset the Coronas I'd slugged down the night before, so with that inspiration in mind I took a deep breath and set off.

"Let's go, fur face, try and keep up, okay?"

I landed on my rear end so quickly I wasn't sure what happened. The source of my crash was yet again Fred, who had pulled in the opposite direction. Second time in one morning I found myself on the ground thanks to my dog.

"What the heck, Fred, what gives? Geeze, if you wanted to go that way you should have just said so." I was attempting to stand up and still hold on to his leash, but he was pulling so hard I was forced to let go. Fred never decides which way we go, ever. Something was wrong with this picture.

"Fine, wait up, we can go this way, where in the world are you going?" I followed as fast as I could, scrambling to my feet and trailing after my dog, who by this time had made it to the nearby sand dune. He stopped suddenly, and began the pitiful howling noises I recognized from another incident on the beach. The sounds made me slow down as I approached him. Fred never howls. Well, only when things are serious and I had really been enjoying myself in the last couple months and it was too early for serious anyways.

The scar on my left thigh, courtesy of the late Chelsea Chester, began to tingle.

Of course I know you're not supposed to speak ill of the dead, but the bitch stabbed me and tried to slice my throat. Now anytime strange things happen my scar feels like it's on fire.

He had his head bent down and was licking the top of the head of another furry creature. Lick, howl, lick as I trained the flashlight on the scene.

"Tusk!" I knelt down and gently placed my hand on the side of the beautiful dog. His breathing was raspy, but his eyes were open. There was a small pool of blood near his hind legs that was rapidly sinking in the sand. "Where's Ms. Betty?"

Ms. Betty is one of my neighbors, a feisty old gal who dedicates her life to the sea turtles. I deduced she and Tusk were out here at this early hour to rescue eggs, but for the life of me I couldn't figure out what happened to Tusk. Fred continued his lick, howl routine and I scanned the sand with my flashlight. To my left the beam picked out a figure face down, and I hurried over.

Ms. Betty was lying at an unusual angle with her own small pool of blood, but this one was near her head. I knelt down and felt the thready pulse at her neck. My breathing slowed a bit. Last time Fred howled like this it was over a dead body. I had no clue what had taken place here, but at least nobody was dead. I was just dialing the police station when a new sound began on the other side of the sand dune. An almost cautious wail that seemed to find more energy as I curiously crept forward.

"Folly Beach police station," answered the voice on the other end of the line.

"Um, Connie? It's Kell. I'm at the beach across from my house. Ms. Betty and Tusk are both hurt. You need to send someone," I said as I made my way towards the noise.

"Oh, no, what happened? McClellan, Jacoby, incident on beach sixteenth block east. Okay, Kell they're on the way," Connie replied. "What is that god-awful sound?"

The wailing was becoming almost unbearably loud and a bit frantic.

The sun was up enough by now so I set the flashlight in the sand and peered around the sand dune.

Nestled in the sand was a wicker basket, and as I got closer I saw that in the basket was the source of the ear piercing squawks. I almost laughed in relief.

"Connie, it's a baby! My gosh, what do I do?"

"A birdie? What kind of bird makes that awful noise?"

"A baby, Connie. Someone left a baby here. Hold on, there's a note pinned to it." I sat down in the sand and gently scooped the tiny infant up in my arms, which had an immediate soothing effect on the child. "The note says I am the spawn of Dax Delaray."

"What? Dax doesn't have any children. And if he does, what's it doing at the beach," Connie asked.

"I have no idea, this is so weird." I jiggled the baby a bit while Fred finally left his position near Tusk and walked past me. He stopped and sat down and started his strange howling again, which the baby didn't care for. I stood up and jiggled a bit more, cradling my cell phone with my shoulder as the infant and Fred competed with each other to see who was loudest.

Amidst the howls and wails my mind slowly focused on what it was seeing. I sort of half fell to my knees and almost dropped the child. Another figure was lying in its very own pool of blood, but judging by the hole in the forehead this one wasn't so lucky. I heaved and upchucked, dropping the phone.

"Kell? Kell, what's happening?" I could make Connie's voice out on the fringes of the surreal setting. "Kell, they're on the way."

I wiped my mouth with the back of my hand and retrieved my phone.

"Connie, I found Dax Delaray," I managed to say. Then little white lights blinked across my field of vision and the first rays of the morning became night.

CHAPTER TWO

"What in the hell have you done this time? You'd think you'd have learned a lesson or two after the last fiasco you created, young lady."

I stared up at the blurred figure wearing a police uniform. "Holy shit, Jacoby!

Dax has a hole in his head! Connie didn't say anyone was dead, but now that I see her I'm not surprised," the voice continued.

"Hey, that's not nice, McClellan. Kell called to report this, we don't know what's going on here yet," said a much kinder voice. This one reached out to touch my shoulder. "Kell, we're here, can you sit up?"

"Shut up, McClellan," I managed to squeak out as my surroundings came in to focus. How dare he talk about me like that, this had absolutely nothing to do with me this time. Besides, I was still holding the infant. "And I didn't drop the baby."

"Baby? What baby? Where'd it come from," asked Officer Mark McClellan as he mopped his forehead. The splotched red spots on his nose were quickly spreading to the rest of his face.

"You okay with that baby, Kell? Just hold on, there. McClellan, check on Tusk," Officer Dan Jacoby instructed his partner as he knelt beside Ms. Betty.

I slowly sat up in the sand with the infant secure in my arms. "Is she alright?"

The shrill ambulance siren in the background came to a halt as three paramedics descended quickly upon the scene. Standing now, I tried again. "Hey, guys, is Ms. Betty alright?"

"Get out of the way, Palevac, just stand over there and hold your baby. And muzzle that mutt of yours," Officer McClellan ordered, boring holes through me with his bulging eyes. I narrowly avoided his bulging stomach as he barreled by.

"Don't talk to my dog like that, and this is not my baby," I shouted. Actually, Fred was getting a bit annoying with the howling, but still. He was standing guard over the body of Dax Delaray, who I was pretty sure wasn't going anywhere. The paramedics were loading Ms. Betty on to a stretcher. I heard a low moan come from her as they lifted her from the sand, and took that as a good sign.

"Hey, don't forget Tusk," I hollered.

McClellan was standing over the injured animal. He shifted his bulk from one foot to the other, reaching with a chubby hand towards the dog. Tusk growled low in his throat and showed his teeth in a rather mean looking snarl. McClellan snatched his hand away quicker than I'd ever seen him do anything.

"You, Palevac, come deal with this dog, I gotta help Jacoby with the body over there," he ordered, backing away from the still snarling Tusk. He tripped over his feet in the soft sand but managed to stay upright as he made his way to Dax Delaray.

Instead of telling him to shut up for the second time I bit my tongue and made my way towards Tusk. Really, I cannot stand to be ordered around, but this did seem to be in the best interest of the animal. McClellan obviously pissed Tusk off, which was a good indication of the dogs' intelligence. Kneeling, I kept the baby up high on my shoulder and whispered.

"Good boy, Tusk. We're going to take you to the hospital, okay? Your mama is fine." His breathing held steady and my voice seemed to comfort him, so I kept up the gentle reassurances and watched the others dealing with the surreal setting I'd stumbled upon.

More officers had arrived, along with our chief of police, Strom Stoney. His blazing blue eyes shot over to me as McClellan and Jacoby filled him in on the situation. Amidst the noise and confusion, I was pretty sure I heard Chief Stoney mutter something along the lines of 'fucking reporter again', which seemed quite unfair but I wasn't saying anything. Not until I talked to my editor.

Two male paramedics appeared by my side and assured me they could handle transporting Tusk without my assistance, so I got out of their way and sat down in the sand, carefully placing the infant in my lap. I'm not much of a baby expert, but deduced this one was pretty new. Dark wisps of hair framed the delicate face and soft brown eyes seemed to be focusing on my right ear. The yellow blanket swaddling the child appeared to be new and was no help in revealing the sex of the baby. I kept my hands off the piece of paper pinned to the blanket declaring this to be Dax Delaray's off-spring. You simply do not touch anything crime related if you can help it. Fingerprints and all that. I'd learned a thing or two from my last dead body. Bodies.

Fred walked dejectedly over and sat beside us with a loud groan. "I know, fur face, I know, here we go again, huh? Don't worry, buddy, we'll go home soon and put this all behind us. I'm sure we won't be needed around much longer," I said, stroking his giant head. I checked the time on my cell phone. "Shit, I better call Alex and let her know what's up, maybe she can call Bonnie and reschedule for me."

My first appointment of the day was with Bonnie McLeod, wife of the mayor and President of Adopt a Pet. I forgot what the topic was this time, but I always give Bonnie my undivided atten-tion. She's a bit eccentric, but we share a love of animals.

I love animals, and Bonnie really, really loves animals. In fact, besides her husband, the only family Bonnie has is furry creatures. As I hit the speed dial connecting me to my editor, I gazed at the tiny infant on my lap. My brain dug for facts about the dead man who had supposedly been this child's father. I quickly disconnected and my phone fell in the sand.

Yep, I consider myself a damn good reporter and Alex would probably chew me out for not calling her right away, but even I knew about the next of kin advisements and all that. I was pretty sure Chief Stoney would chase me out of town if it was discovered

I'd called my editor. My morning appointment was not an issue anymore. I felt like smacking my forehead. Bonnie McLeod did have family of the human variety, and I certainly wasn't going to be the one to advise her that her brother was dead and she might be an aunt.

CHAPTER THREE

"Ms. Palevac!" The sound of my own name being shrieked across the sand snapped me out of my soon to be catatonic state. I stared at my phone. I stared at the baby. Fred stared at me. The lapping of the waves on shore was soothing, and for a moment I tried to concentrate on the steady in and out of the tide. Sort of like, breathe in, breathe out. If I closed my eyes it actually seemed like a little bit of yoga by the beach. Somewhere out there a whole lot of people were making a whole lot of noise but not me. Me, I was just trying to breathe.

"Palevac! Don't bore me with the details of what the hell you're doing in the middle of this mess," Chief Strom Stoney descended on me so fast I forgot to breathe and started to hiccup. Fred hates this. He takes my hiccups as a sign of failure, and quickly tucked his head under my armpit and tried to hide. "Get your ass to the station and make a full report."

Even though my ass was currently sitting in the sand, I reminded myself Chief Stoney is a short little guy, and if I could just stand up we'd be seeing eye to eye. First thing was to open my eyes, which worked alright, but the standing part was a bit trickier, what with a baby in my lap and Fred under my armpit. I held my breath in an attempt to dispel the hiccups.

"Chief Stoney, there's really no reason to yell at me, I just….." I tried.

"Don't push me young lady," the chief said. He swept his eyes over the scene. All parties involved were being removed from the beach. Maybe if I sat still they'd get a stretcher for me, too.

Chief Stoney was through with me. I deduced this as I watched him turn his back and move off in the other direction. Fred peeked out from my armpit and bravely held his head high as we both pretty much figured out we were on our own.

"Well, fur face, another day in paradise, huh? Let's get up and get out of here," I said. Fred didn't say anything, but his eyes reflected the same dazed feeling I was experiencing. "Let me just grab this baby here and we're off."

We silently made our way back over the sand dunes to the road. It was so quiet now, the hush of the early morning back so quickly it was as if nothing out of the ordinary had taken place. The sun was up by now and warmed my back as we walked across the street.

Squealing tires interrupted the silence as a moving vehicle barreled down on us and came to a sudden halt about one foot from my left leg. I hugged the baby to my chest and lunged forward, whipping around to see my dog growling at a bright blue Jeep just inches from his face. Fred surprises me like that at times. Just when

I think he's the biggest scaredy cat he gets all Rambo-like and confronts things. Like cars.

"For the love of God, Kell! What in the name of all that is holy are you doin' steppin' out in to the road like that? You could be killed," hollered the voice of my dear best friend Siobhan Mulvaney. "I know you get spacey at times, girl, but you really need to open your eyes!"

I stared at the source of the kind words. Siobhan was behind the wheel of her Jeep with her unending length of reddish hair hanging out the window as she addressed me. Me, her best friend, whom she had just about run over. But of course, this was all my fault. To top things off the baby was now wailing at a high speed rate.

"You know, Siobhan, you drive entirely too fast," I retorted, jiggling the infant as I spoke. "Come, Fred, get out of the way before she forgets to keep her foot on the pedal and squishes you."

The jiggly thing wasn't doing much. In the utter confusion of the morning I seemed to have forgotten I was left alone with a child. Really, the thing had been so quiet. Not anymore. The wails intensified and Fred began howling in response.

'My, isn't someone in a fine mood this morning. I don't know what your problem is, Kell, but don't be takin' it out on me. I'm going to park in front of your house. And, by the way, you're holding a baby."

"No shit," I yelled at the car as Siobhan backed up. Of course I was holding a baby. Any idiot could see that. The question was why did the people in charge of this mess leave the papoose with me?

Fred and I shuffled slowly to our house. "Okay, smart dog, how is it that we were left with this," I asked. The baby and Fred both howled in response.

I live in the bottom half of a wonderful house, complete with upstairs neighbors who keep things from getting lonely. Ludmilla Dubrov and her teenage son, Elbert, are permanent fixtures, while Ludmilla's questionable boyfriend Murphy comes and goes.

Siobhan was already at my front door retrieving my keys from underneath the hibiscus plant. By the time Fred and I walked inside she had plopped down on my sofa and had her feet on the oak-planked coffee table.

"Get your feet off my table," I snapped, setting the crying bundle in her lap and pushing her cowboy boots off the beautiful oak.

Siobhan, for once in her life, seemed speechless as she stared at the wailing child. Her slender fingers cautiously stroked the newborn's cheek. I stopped and sat down beside her, gazing at the baby. Fred stood next to me and with his giant tongue began to gently lick the fuzzy wisps of hair on top of the infant's head. Okay, nobody was going to believe this grooming technique would produce such a cute mohawk, but there was no denying the calmness that resulted. No more crying.

"So, are you going to tell me where you found this? This is not the same as rescuing baby squirrels, you know. This is a human we have here," Siobhan said. "By the way, is it a boy or a girl?"

"Of course I realize this is a human, and I have no idea what kind, and nor, for that matter, did I ask to keep it."

"Okay, don't go getting all testy with me, girl. The only reason I'm even here is because Alex called me and said there was some sort of commotion going on. Sent me to get photos of whatever it was," Siobhan said.

In her defense I will say my rather sassy friend is an excellent photographer, the best one we have at *The Archipelago*. Our editor, Alex DeWinter has an uncanny ability to smell a story even if it is taking place in the wee morning hours. Either that or the woman was secretly wire tapping the police station's radio waves.

"Listen, I really have to tell you what's going on," I said, standing back up. I walked over to the large cage in the corner and lifted off the blanket.

"Wanna have sex?"

"For the millionth time, no," I shouted back at Blackbeard, my fairly large, colorful parrot whom I received as a gift from Murphy. According to Murphy, the bird's previous owner was a sea captain who couldn't keep Blackbeard at the retirement center he now called home. Of course Murphy thought of me, lover of all animals, and bestowed the questionable present upon me a few months back.

"Show me your knockers," Blackbeard demanded. Sampson snuck up behind the cage and leaped to the top, swishing his long black tail and swiping at the bird with pointy claws.

"Show some manners or I'll cover you back up. Anyways, wait until you hear this," I continued, proceeding to fill Siobhan in on the implausible events of the morning.

"Ah, this is a mystical child, then, sort of like Moses being left in the basket, or the babies the fairies steal from the forest," she claimed, looking at the now sleeping baby with a sort of reverence.

I rolled my eyes. Siobhan is quite caught up in her Celtic past, her present belief in the dream world and quite possibly who she would come back as in the future. I try not to get too involved with her ramblings. And she thinks *I'm* spacey.

"Actually, this one seems to be at the center of a murder mystery. I did mention the note stating this is Dax Delaray's child. You know, the dead guy?"

"And Dax is Bonnie's brother, although hardly anyone knows that because she doesn't do the human thing much," Siobhan noted.

"Who in the world is going to tell her what happened," I fretted, pacing the floor. "I was supposed to meet her this morning. What a mess."

"Yeah, I saw Bonnie last evening at the market, she said she was meeting you here early," Siobhan declared. "Like at 7:30." She glanced at her watch. "Which would be right about now."

Okay, so this was where I was supposed to meet Bonnie. Here. At my house. I stopped pacing. "Surely someone has reached her by now." I rubbed my scar.

The doorbell rang. Siobhan and I stared at each other.

"Or maybe not," she said.

CHAPTER FOUR

If the doorbell rang one more time I was going to scream. Siobhan and I stared at each other some more.

"Well, answer the door, will you? That's normally what people do when the bell rings," Siobhan said. Despite her smart tongue she did appear a bit pale beneath her freckles.

Okay, answer the door. Then what? Say hello, Bonnie, how are you, lovely shirt you're wearing, and oh, by the way, I do believe your brother took a bullet to the brain. Yep, not only that but here, this is your niece. Nephew. I really should figure out if the child was male or female. Probably when it came time to change a diaper the mystery would be revealed. Which made me remember I didn't have any diapers. And what did the baby eat? Surely the poor thing was getting hungry.

"Kell!" The bell had stopped ringing and now my front door was being assaulted with some serious banging. "Open the door, I know you're in there, and Siobhan, too."

I snapped out of it and practically sank to the floor with relief. "It's Mid."

"Of course it's Middleton, he always knows when you've done something," Siobhan said as some of the color returned to her face. "So, open the door already, the baby is going to wake up."

I stuck my tongue out at her and did as instructed. Middleton Langdon Calhoun brushed past me so quickly I barely caught a waft of his trademark citrusy scent, mixed in with the smell of salty air.

"Okay, what the hell is going on," he demanded.

Mid is my best friend, well, along with Siobhan, and has been rescuing me from all sorts of incidences since I was about twelve years old. He exudes an air of such confidence that it typically infects the rest of us. I felt myself standing up straighter.

"Well, golly gee, good morning to you, too."

"Top of the mornin' and all that, Mid," Siobhan echoed.

He began pacing the room, which I immediately recognized as a sign he was highly agitated. Normally Mid remains calm, cool and collected. Normally I'm the one pacing.

I sat next to Siobhan on the couch and together we observed our mutual buddy. His brown hair was windswept, which meant he was riding with the top down on his mustang. Mid's on the tall side of six feet, slim but powerfully built, with the refined sophistication and cool elegance of a southern gentleman born into one of Charleston's most well-bred families. I've always admired his ability to remain calm.

"This is definitely not the time for pleasantries, ladies," he said. "Kell, for the hundredth time, why make little problems when you can create a holocaust? The chief filled me in."

"What? What did he say? Why did he contact you?" I felt myself sinking into the couch.

"I'm the crime reporter, remember? And I contacted him," Mid said. His voice usually sounds like steel wrapped in silk but right now I sensed an edge of desperation. "Please tell me there is absolutely nothing connecting you with this latest incident."

"Me? Of course not, I just seem to be one of the only people on this island who gets up early in the morning, which is apparently when most crimes are committed around here," I stated. "Maybe you should try it, Mid, getting up early. You are the crime reporter, after all."

"And you're the reporter for this town, which is beginning to seem like not such a great idea," Mid said. "I should call your parents and let them know what's going on."

I was about to reply with another smart aleck remark when the hilarity of his comment struck me. Call my parents? The people who sent me down the Amazon river in a canoe? Please. They think this tiny town is the safest place I've ever lived. Well, they do worry about rednecks, who they simply do not understand. But that's another story.

Middleton grinned. "Okay, so that's not an option. But seriously, Kell, what in the world were you doing? You find an injured dog and his injured owner, who are both going to be fine, by the way. Then to top it off you just so happen to discover a dead man with a bullet in his head."

"Don't forget the baby," Siobhan interjected. "She brought home a baby, too, Mid."

"You people are starting to get on my nerves! What was I supposed to do, leave it in the sand?"

"Wait a minute. The chief didn't say anything about a baby. What baby," Mid asked.

"This little mite here, so sweet, don't you think," Siobhan replied, holding the infant out for inspection. "Kell seems to think it's Dax's child, although I don't know how she figured that out so fast."

Mid's jaw muscles seemed to be attempting to contain some serious clenched teeth. "From the beginning, Kell. Where did you get the baby? Why do you think it belongs to Dax? A baby! This is not the same as rescuing squirrels."

"I already told her that," Siobhan agreed.

I pinched the bridge of my nose. Hard. This usually helps to stave off the headaches these two induce. Maybe it was time for new best friends.

"Stop already! The baby was on the beach in a basket and had a note pinned on saying it was Dax's. I'm sure Chief Stoney has the note, but nobody seemed too interested in the kid, so I was sort of left with it. Geeze," I said.

The bell rang again and I took the moment to flounce away from the both of them and looked out the window. Parked out front were the Chief's police cruiser and two other official looking vehicles. I opened the door.

"Palevac, I certainly hope that child is in good condition. Who gave you permission to cart it over here to your house," Chief Stoney demanded. He marched past me with two women in tow. One had a tight face that was drained of color and a tangerine pouf for hair. Her lips were pursed suspiciously and I was pretty sure her eyebrows were drawn on. She had on a mustard brown tunic over a maroon shirt. All in all, not a pretty picture.

"Kell Palevac, meet Joyce Price from the Department of Social Services. You already know Lurleen."

I shook hands with the DSS lady and smiled at Lurleen Higgenbottom. She smiled back. Joyce from DSS did not.

Chief Stoney made the introductions to the rest in the room while Joyce plucked the sleeping baby from Siobhan's arms. The movement caused the child to wake up and squawk a protesting wail. Rather expertly, Joyce placed the child on its back and unwrapped the soft blanket. Before any of us could figure out what was happening, she'd removed the small diaper.

"We have a little girl," she announced as if the rest of us couldn't have come to the same conclusion. She quickly produced a clean diaper from the bag she was carrying and wrapped the baby up again.

"First of all, Chief, the only reason I have it, or her, is because everyone left," I explained.

"There is no time to indulge ourselves in your ramblings and excuses," Chief Stoney said. "Now, this is what is going to happen."

I watched his mouth move while I conjured up all sorts of intelligent comebacks. While I was thinking he was yakking about

DNA tests and a bunch of other stuff. I did manage to make out that Lurleen would be caring for the child while everything was sorted out. Turns out she's a foster parent.

"And nobody can locate Bonnie. I understand she had an early meeting with you," the Chief stared at me accusingly.

This is the part I simply can't stand when things fall apart around here. Everyone thinks I did something. Okay, I give, I've got Bonnie locked up in the closet. Is that what he thought?

"She was due here at 7:30, but I haven't heard from her. Let me see if I can reach her," I said, unclipping my cell from my shorts. The screen indicated I'd missed one text message.

"Kell," it read. "Please forgive me for missing our appointment. I've had a horrible night. Going to take my kayak out, leaving phone off. Need peace. Sure you'll hear about it all soon. Bonnie."

I gulped. Bonnie never, ever is without her phone. What did this mean? Did she already know about Dax? But how could she? I was the one who found him. Or was I?

CHAPTER FIVE

A vague hazy sensation enveloped me as I watched the Chief, DSS lady, Lurleen and the infant exit through my front door. I was never so happy to see people leave. Well, not Lurleen or the baby, but certainly tangerine head. And definitely Chief Stoney. I wasn't letting on about my message from Bonnie until I spoke with her husband. In fact, I wasn't telling anyone.

"What in the hell are they all doing here," I asked in disbelief as my editor's black Saab screeched to a halt outside. Alex expertly exited on four-inch spiked heels and slammed the door. From the backseat emerged Holly Chesnut and Kenneth Linski, two of my dear co-workers. Since my last brush with death Kenneth and I were at least on speaking terms. He's a bit emotional like that. Holly, she's still a bitch. I'm sorry, but I simply have no good things to say about the girl.

"Come on people, step it up! We have a story to cover! Move it, move it, move it," Alex barked like an ornery drill instructor. Holly and Kenneth scurried faster and came inside with Alex on their heels. "Everyone take a seat and take notes!"

I must have missed the memo saying the party was at my house this morning. Did these people know I hadn't even showered yet? While everyone found a seat Fred and I stood and stared at the assembled group. Apparently defeated, Fred sat down on the floor. Since there weren't any seats left for me, I sat next to him.

"Show me your knockers!"

Alex DeWinter whirled around so fast I thought her head was going to pop off. "You! You mouthy little bird, shut up! I don't have time for your insults."

"Screw you!" My eyes widened and Fred tilted his head sideways. Blackbeard had never said that before, but then again, dealing with Alex does bring out the worst in most people.

I jumped up and covered his cage before Alex scratched him with one of her pointed fingernails. "Um, just exactly what are we all doing here? At my house?"

Holly had squeezed herself in between Mid and Siobhan on the couch, pressing her legs against Mid's. I glared at him. Holly smirked and fluffed her auburn curls. "Why, we're here to work. Remember work, Kell? Something you're supposed to do instead of creating drama all the time," she said in her perfect southern drawl. She twirled a curl with a fingertip painted blood red. I thought about punching her.

"Geeze, Holly, can you bag it for once," asked Linski, his hands snatching bits of spiked hair and pulling them up. He does this when he's upset. "Someone's been murdered."

"Exactly, and once again Kell laid claim to the dead body," Holly retorted. "I suppose she gets to cover this story, too."

I felt my fist curling up and Mid shot me a warning glance. I punched Holly once before, back in college. It had been awhile.

"Just because I found a dead person doesn't mean it's mine, you moron. Really, Holly, I wish you'd found Dax. Bullet hole straight through the forehead. Blood and guts and all that good stuff."

I secretly grinned while Holly grew white and leaned over towards Mid. Siobhan rolled her eyes at me.

Alex, on the other hand, was turning red. "Children, you are all testing my nerves right now. Right down to the very last nerve," she shouted.

Someone, probably Ludmilla, banged on my ceiling from above. This is our way of letting each other know things were getting too loud. Usually I'm the one banging, especially when Murphy's in town.

We all watched as Alex composed herself by counting to ten. She did it again. Linski coughed and Siobhan wiggled in her seat. I shut up.

Alex took a deep breath. "As you all know, an important member of our community was found dead. Dax Delaray was many things. A restaurant owner, a triathalete and a Folly Beach local. This story will be on the front page of tomorrow's paper."

Mid raised his hand. "Alex? What angle do you want me to take on the murder?"

I swear Alex DeWinter had a shit-eating grin on her face, but since she's so ladylike I knew this wasn't possible.

"Well, Middleton, this will be a big article. Big. Since you are the crime reporter, you will be focusing on that aspect. Kell, since you are the reporter for Folly, you will focus on his life here," she said. "Kenneth, as the sports writer, your angle will be Dax's love for fitness. Holly, as the foods writer you will elaborate on Dax's restaurant, The Seaside Grill. Siobhan, I'm assigning you to cover all photos necessary."

Okay, so the shit-eating grin did exist. Alex had just succeeded in assigning a story to all of us. Which meant we had to work together.

From this point everything happened so fast I wasn't sure I was alone until my front door slammed. Holly flounced and pouted, Linski whined, Siobhan, damn her, laughed, I tried to explain how this was never going to work and Mid did nothing.

For the second time today Fred rolled over on his back and stuck his legs up in the air. The dead dog trick. I just might try it.

CHAPTER SIX

I took a shower so fast the mirror in my bathroom didn't even have time to steam up. Usually I like to spend longer in my oasis-like setting, but today my hair didn't even get washed. Then again, I didn't crack a sweat because I didn't get to run because I just so happened to live in a town that was getting odder by the minute.

Fred and Sampson were curled up together on my bed, watching me as I scurried around. "I know you guys are hungry, just a few more minutes, okay?"

Nothing was where it was supposed to be, which is fairly typical for me because I can't seem to put my clothes away. I snagged the jeans I wore the night before off the floor and shook them out. "These are clean, no problem, now a shirt," I said, darting over to my closet. "Shit!"

I tripped over a small pile of books on the floor next to my bed and barely escaped bodily injury as I landed on top of my animals. Sampson hissed in annoyance. Fred didn't seem to feel me when I crashed on top of him. Rolling over, I laid on my back and stared at the ceiling.

Somewhere I remember reading that if you're feeling anxious you should stare at the ceiling and calmness would ensue. Breathe in, breathe out. What should I do? Okay, so Bonnie and Dax didn't have a close relationship. In fact, now that I was staring at the ceiling a whole bunch of thoughts were coming to me. Bonnie referring to her brother as a worthless womanizer. Breathe in, breathe out. Dax drunkenly interrupting a city council meeting and calling the Mayor a lush. Bonnie tossing a drink at Dax one night at The Coast because he was wearing a fur-trimmed cap. My scar began to throb. I sat up.

"Screw the ceiling technique," I shouted. Fred opened one eye and yawned. Someone pounded on the ceiling from above. "Calm down, Ludmilla! Hit the Stoli bottle if I'm bothering you so much."

Okay, so just because Bonnie and Dax didn't have the healthiest of sibling sentiments towards one another did not mean Bonnie would have killed him. Absolutely not. There had to be an explanation as to why Bonnie disappeared the same night her brother was found dead. By me.

I scurried to the closet and flung open the door. Clothes. Someone should really come over and organize my clothes. I grabbed the pair of jeans again, put them on and picked out one of the many colored v-neck t-shirts my mom recently sent me from Brasil. Supposedly all sales of these exact shirts benefited the rainforests, which was pretty cool since I now owned one in just about every color of the rainbow. I shrugged myself into a shade of blue, added my favorite belt and slipped on sandals.

In the bathroom I gathered my mess of hair in to a ponytail and powdered my nose. There really wasn't time to primp today, which was fine by me. My giant black bag holding all my gear was waiting for me. I grabbed my keys and snatched the towel off of the bird's cage so he could stay awake and sleep at night.

"Try to learn some nice words today, Blackbeard," I instructed the parrot, locking my door behind me as I made it outside.

"I'm horny!"

"Horny is not a nice word," I shouted back and plowed into something blocking the way to my car.

"Why isn't horny a nice word, Kell? It's what people do who get mad in traffic and beep their horns a lot, but my mom says it's the people who aren't nice. It's not the word's fault," explained my favorite neighbor Elbert. "Now, fucking motherfucker is not nice. My mom says I can't call Murphy that anymore."

Elbie's hair was a little on the long side and matted down on top. He's tall so I had to crane my neck back to see his face. He's also plagued by teenage acne and the view wasn't pretty, so I looked at my car and unlocked the door.

"Don't worry about it, Elbie, I was talking to Blackbeard," I said, tossing my bag inside.

Elbie snickered. He twirled a finger in circles next to his temple. "You can't talk to animals, Kell. Even I know that. You can't talk to people who aren't there, either. My mom told me that one."

I got in my Toyota Four-Runner and rolled down the window. "We'll talk about all this later, okay Elbie? I have to go, I'm in a hurry, so bye."

"Where you going, Kell! I wanna come with you," Elbie shouted as I pulled off. "Come back, Kell, you never let me come with you!"

"I am on my way to see the Mayor of this psycho town," I muttered. Okay, now I was talking to myself. "And he better have some answers."

CHAPTER SEVEN

George and Bonnie McLeod's house is a few blocks away from mine. Head towards town, take a right on Tenth Street and keep going until you hit the marsh, which keeps you from falling in to the Folly River. Some people who come to Folly are rather surprised we're literally surrounded by water. They need to be reminded we are an island, after all. Me, I love it. The idea of being landlocked literally makes me panic.

My tires crunched over the oyster shell driveway. An army of dogs in various shapes and sizes emerged from the garage and began announcing my arrival. I've been to this house plenty of times, so I knew from experience the best thing was to forge a path through the pack and make it to the front door.

"Hey ya'll, how's things in doggie world today," I asked, scratching an ear here and there. Nobody snarled or growled but I was practically licked to death by the time I reached the house. "Where's your daddy?"

The doorbell produced no sign of George McLeod, so I walked around back trailed by half the animal kingdom. I felt kind of like the Pied Piper. "Alright, furry ones, where's he at?"

I raised my hand to shield the sun and squinted towards the end of the 300 foot dock extending through the marsh. Mayor McLeod was sitting on a bench looking out over the water. I took a deep breath and began the trek to reach him. The dogs trailed behind me in a straight line, and I noticed a few cats straggling along behind them. Good thing we all kept it single file, these docks are just about wide enough for one person. And I still can't figure out why they put a wooden railing down one entire side but leave the other side open. Some of these suckers have no railings at all, so I considered myself lucky to be half safe.

After what felt like an hour I was finally closing in on the end of the dock. "Hey, Mayor? Mayor McLeod, hi, it's Kell Palevac."

He turned and gave me a little nod, patting the bench beside him. I took the invitation and sat down. The dogs kept going and silently dove off the dock one by one, splashing in to the water below.

"How do they get back up on the dock," I asked.

"Don't. They swim back towards the house and muck through the pluff mud," the Mayor replied. "One little guy was stuck in the stuff for two days before I found him." The cats had perched themselves on the railing, watching with disdain as their furry counterparts frolicked.

The Mayor and I sat in silence for a little while. Even at this early hour boats sped by, and the occasional jet ski zipped across the water.

"Dolphins!" I stood up and shouted excitedly, pointing at the water. "Sorry," I said, sitting down again. No matter how many times I see them it still feels like spotting a famous celebrity or something.

George McLeod is normally an imposing figure with a slightly crooked nose that gives him a kind of rugged geniality. Today his body looked to be about as limp as filleted fish. He sighed gustily.

"Well, I guess I know why you're here. Nothing is private in this town for very long," he said, patting his shirt in an absent searching motion. I pointed to the top of his head.

Mayor McLeod retrieved his glasses and cleaned them with a corner of his shirt. With another heavy sigh he put them on and stared out at the water.

I cleared my throat. "Have you been able to reach your wife, sir?"

His voice cracked with a sardonic weariness. "Reach my wife? She took off in her kayak. She certainly has nothing to say to me right about now."

"Yes, but, surely we can find her somehow. Do you know where she was heading?"

"The last thing I heard her shouting was she was going far away from me, so that could be just about anywhere. I know my wife, Ms. Palevac. When she gets mad it's best to stay out of the way."

My chest flickered with little butterflies. "So, she was pretty mad."

"Ha! Furious is more like it," the Mayor shouted.

Oops. Maybe I shouldn't have come alone. I was, after all, out in the middle of the marsh with a fairly angry man.

"I would have told her but I knew she would never understand," he continued, standing up. 'She had to hear it through the island's grapevine, and you know how that goes. All the details, not all the facts."

A confusing rush of anticipation and dread enveloped me. "But why? Why do something so awful? This doesn't sound like Bonnie at all," I said, shaking my head.

The Mayor threw his head back and unleashed something between a howl and a laugh. His mouth lifted in a menacing, sarcastic smile. "Why, I thought you knew my wife, Ms. Palevac. In fact, you're as much of an animal nut as she is, aren't you?"

I kept my voice flat and neutral. "What does any of that have to do with Dax Delaray?"

This time the Mayor snorted. "That sorry excuse for a brother-in-law is probably the fool who told her. You think he'd understand, he did grow up in the same house as Bonnie, he knows how she gets."

Okay, definitely not on the same page. I stood up and looked at George McLeod. His eyebrows were knitted together in a look of helplessness.

"Just tell me what happened," I said gently.

His sobs startled the cats, who were lounging in the morning sunshine. They all looked pretty pissed off. "I ate a cheeseburger!

One! Well, okay, one that anyone knew about. I can't take it anymore!"

I scrunched up my nose and blinked a couple times. Bonnie and George are vegetarians. Never eat anything with a face and all that. Me, I love animals. I just don't think about them while I'm eating.

"So, she got angry because she found out you ate meat," I stated, pacing the dock. "Maybe you aren't cut out to be a vegetarian."

"After thirty-five years a man needs some real sustenance," the Mayor shouted.

"Calm down, Mayor, I completely understand. The part I don't understand is how Dax figures in to all of this?"

"Why do you keep bringing that knucklehead up? He's not a vegetarian, oh, no, he can eat whatever the hell he wants!"

Considering the man was dead I begged to differ but I've learned to choose my battles. Why was the Mayor talking about Dax like he was still among the living?

I heard the dock creaking and looked over my shoulder. Chief Stoney and some man I didn't recognize were walking in our direction.

"What in the hell does he want? I'm not showing up today, he can play Mayor if he wants," Mayor McLeod said in a rather pouty little voice.

Understanding was seeping in slowly. "You haven't talked to anyone yet today, Mayor?"

He shook his head. "No, after Bonnie left I couldn't sleep so I went for a walk and then came out here. Haven't been near a phone. Why, did they find her? Is she okay?"

The Chief was getting pretty close and I really considered jumping in after the dogs and mucking it back to shore to avoid him. With my luck I'd get stuck in the pluff mud and nobody would find me even after two days. I held my ground.

"Yes, Chief Stoney, what brings you to my property on this early morning," bellowed Mayor McLeod.

It was my turn to do some heavy duty sighing.

CHAPTER EIGHT

My feet were on my desk, I was leaning back in my chair and I still had my shades on. Through this false sense of security I could see my coworkers working on their portions of the story slated for tomorrow's front page. Linski was pecking away feverishly on his keyboard. I knew he'd have his section done in no time. Holly chewed on one of her curls. I was hoping she'd cough up a hairball.

"Kell, I don't see you working, I'd hate for you to ruin this whole article for the rest of us by not doing your part," Holly said, stretching her slender neck from side to side.

Maybe I could help her out and just snap it. One quick yank. The idea made me grin.

'I certainly wouldn't smile," she continued. "Alex wants us to all have our parts complete so she can combine them by this afternoon."

Mid was pacing with his cell phone to his ear. He pretended he wasn't listening to Holly but I could tell he was paying attention by the worried looks he was sending my way.

"It's amazing you actually are still employed here. Rumor has it the Chief finds it highly suspicious you're the only one finding dead people on the island," Holly intoned, twirling the now soggy curl around her finger.

The girl really doesn't know when to shut the hell up. I slowly removed my feet from their comfortable resting place. Mid had stopped pacing and was watching me.

"Middleton, dear, your little underling just may be in danger of losing her job if she doesn't get started. This is an important story, you know," Holly said.

I got up, walked the few feet to her desk, and squatted down so I was on her level. She raised her eyebrows.

"You know, Holly, rumor has it this isn't the end of the dead bodies," I said. "Yep, I heard the killer is searching right now for his next victim. I'm recommending you."

Holly paled visibly, which is always cool. I lowered my shades and stared her down. "You better hurry on the story there, just in case you aren't around anymore. Killer and all."

Holly stood up so fast her chair fell over. "Stop it! You are such an evil bitch, Kell Palevac!"

I stood up next to her. "And you're the most annoying excuse for a person I've ever seen. Southern belle, my ass."

She really shouldn't have shoved me. It was actually a sissy sort of shove, but still. Mid grabbed my clenched fist right before it made contact with her face.

"Ladies, and I use the word loosely, settle down," he said. He had my arm around my back, but I shrugged him off and took a step in Holly's direction.

"Middleton," she squeaked, so he stepped in front of me. I could see Holly trembling a little behind him. "Get her away from me!"

I decided to do the mature thing, so I peeked around Mid. "Holly, I'm going to pretend you don't exist anymore, which, hey, just might come true with a killer out there," I said. "So have a nice life. Or die. I don't care."

I grabbed my bag and pushed past Mid. "I can't work with this whiney ass idiot around, I'm outta here."

"What about your part of the article," Mid asked.

"I'll do it on my laptop," I hollered. As I was making my way to the front door I could still hear Holly moaning.

"I'm a lady, you know that, Middleton. She's just so, well, so not a lady, it simply brings out the worst in me."

I paused near our receptionist's desk. Myra Glass quickly got up from her seat and held the door open for me.

"Go, dear, go. Just go," she said a bit nervously. "We all know Holly is high strung."

I contemplated rushing back inside and pouncing on the bothersome Holly but remembered she didn't exist anymore. "Bye, Myra."

The door slammed behind me. I stalked off down Center Street, willing Holly out of my head. I tried to think about other things, like poor Mayor McLeod. He wasn't too upset when the Chief informed him about Dax Delaray, but he worked himself in to a tizzy when he found out Bonnie might be an aunt. He was muttering some nonsense like please, not a human when I left the dock.

The air was warm and breezy as I made my way towards the ocean, passing the various little shops and restaurants in my town. A few blocks away a tall reddish haired woman was gesturing wildly with her hands and hollering at someone sitting on a bench.

What was Siobhan doing outside of The Coast?

The person on the bench got up. He looked like a huge block from where I was at. Cyrus, my good buddy biker pal, was clearly visible even from here. He stands out in any crowd you put him in, and right then Siobhan grabbed his arm and pulled him with her in to The Coast.

Maybe it was noon. It was most definitely five o'clock somewhere. I picked up my pace and covered the last couple blocks in a flash, ready to join my friends at my favorite watering hole.

CHAPTER NINE

I pulled open the door to The Coast and peered inside. It always takes my eyes a few seconds to adjust to the darkness when I come here in the daytime, which isn't too often. Usually I save an outing to The Coast for evenings, but, hey, the way my day was going I probably deserved a break.

You rarely find tourists here, but it sure is a great place to track down the locals. I recognized a few faces bellying up to the bar at lunchtime. I smiled and waved and hurried past Judge Preston Brooks, who cannot stand me. It's rather silly, really, but since he is a judge and all I try to stay out of his way.

"You forgot to greet the good Judge, Kell," hollered a familiar voice from the other side of the bar.

"Shut up, will you," I hissed at Siobhan as I planted myself on the stool next to her.

Cyrus stood up from the barstool on her other side. "Where'ya been hidin' at, little lady," he asked, engulfing me in a giant bear hug.

He stood up to his full height of about 6'3" and puffed out his strong chest. "That there judge botherin' you? I know a few people, if you get my drift."

I was pretty sure through the smoky haze Judge Brooks was trying to bore holes through me with his eyes. "Hush, sit back down, Cyrus." He's a bouncer at The Coast and takes his job very seriously.

"Whatever do you mean, you know people? You're the people, silly," Siobhan giggled. "Another martini, extra olives."

Krissy was the bartender on duty today. She's my favorite. Her brown dreadlocks were gathered together with a bandana and she had on so much silver jewelry she jingled. She took the empty glass.

"What's ya havin', girl," she asked me.

I had no idea what Siobhan was up to at this time of day, but it looked like this might be lunch. "Does a Bloody Mary have any nutritional value?"

Krissy pursed her lips. "Hmm, well, sure. Tomatoes. And we can load it up with celery and jalapenos. Lots of veggies."

"Okay," I agreed.

"The olives are why I'm having martinis," added Siobhan. "Very nutritious."

A loud burp emerged from my buddy Cyrus. "I'm havin' beer."

Okay, so now that we were done with our lunch selections I posed the question. "What in the hell are we doing here? We're supposed to be working." I took a long sip of the drink Krissy placed before me. Delicious. "Or maybe not."

Siobhan knocked back her second martini and slammed the glass down on the bar. "Hit me again, Krissy girl."

"Um, Siobhan," I asked, sipping on my drink. "What are we doing?"

My kind of out of control friend narrowed her green eyes. "Drinking."

"Yeah, Kell, don't be a party pooper, I'm always tellin' ya there's too much working going on with you," Cyrus agreed.

"Okay, I get that we're drinking in the middle of the day, but why?"

Cyrus was shaking his head side to side and making little silent no's at me with his lips. Siobhan speared an olive with her toothpick and chomped it. Hard.

"Kell, my dear best friend, I have told you about my siblings, correct? All those smashing brothers and sisters of mine tucked away far, far away in Ireland," she asked.

"Well, sure, I know there are eight of you and all," I replied. Cyrus was leaning forward on his barstool and making strange faces at me. "What? Geeze, Cyrus, talk already."

Siobhan ignored both of us and continued with her rather one sided discussion.

"Yes, so far away, which is how I've liked it all these years, had enough of those people crammed together," she rambled. "Visit when I can. None of them ever wanted to leave, oh no, but now? Just call me out of the blue and say you're flying on over." Her martini glass was empty again and she held it up to Krissy. This was going to be her fourth and I opened my mouth to comment but Krissy met my eyes and shook her head. Okay, pick your fights and all that.

"Out of all of them, the whole bloody lot, and who has to decide to come for a visit? Well, who do you think," Siobhan's voice was escalating and all eyes around the bar were on her.

I scrambled around in my brain trying to remember some of the names. Declan, Finn, Chloe or Clea or something like that.

"Maeve!" Siobhan declared, pounding her fist on the hard wood.

"Maeve!" I decided the best thing to do was just agree with her. My spicy beverage was empty and I waved the glass at Krissy.

"My baby sister Maeve. Do you know I was there when she was born? Five years old I was, and Da wanted all the rest of us there because he swore this would be the last," Siobhan said. "So there we were, all seven of us crowded in the room and finally the baby was born. Wasn't making a peep, so the good doctor smacked her on the butt, and did she cry? Nope. She giggled. Doctor about dropped her on her head, he was so shocked."

The audience at the bar was rapt by now. I cleared my throat. "Um, giggled? Newborns don't do that, do they?"

Siobhan gave me a withering look. "I'm trying to tell you about Maeve."

"Fine, fine, continue," I waved a hand at her.

"Her hair was black as the night, and her eyes the strangest violet. Look at me," Siobhan commanded. "Red hair, green eyes, right? Just like the rest of us. Then Maeve. Black Irish."

I'd always thought they were all redheads. Then again, I'd never heard about Maeve before. I sipped my drink and paid attention.

"Right from the start we knew there was something about her. Over the years the whole village knew, too. Maeve mesmerized everyone, she was like an old soul in a child's body. By the time she was fourteen the entire town was in love with the girl," Siobhan continued. "Maybe if my parents had chosen a suitable name things would have been different."

Cyrus spoke up. "Sure sounds like a strange name to me," he agreed. "But so's your name, Siobhan."

A ray of light broke through the darkness and we all shielded our eyes, like vampires caught in the daybreak. Mid stood in the doorway.

"Hurry up 'n siddown, Mid," Scary Harry said from his barstool. "We're listening to a story here."

Middleton came around the bar and stared at me. "What in the hell is this, Kell? I've been looking for you. You're supposed to be working."

"Shut up," the whole room shouted at once. I smiled at Mid and shrugged my shoulders. Cyrus stood up and took hold of Mid's arm and sort of forced him on to the barstool next to him.

"Drink up will ya man, people are sober over in Indiana," Cyrus said.

"I think it's India, Cyrus," Mid responded with that little edge to his voice he gets when forced to deal with Cyrus.

"Yep, probably there, too," Cyrus agreed.

Once we were all settled again Siobhan continued her story. "In ancient Gaelic her name means the cause of great intoxication, or she who makes men drunk."

Around the bar people were nodding their approval and murmuring amongst themselves.

"Really? Cool," commented Cyrus. "Quite down, the lady is trying to talk here."

Siobhan kissed his cheek. "Thank-you, darlin' boy." I could tell she was on her way to being quite sauced but, hey, she's a grown adult. Not my problem. I chewed a celery stick.

"She certainly didn't do much to help matters. Maeve was never promiscuous, just rather innocently lethal. Like our Ma would tell us never be caught with holey underwear on. Maeve was sent home from kindergarten one day because her teacher discovered she was bear naked under her dress," Siobhan related. "Told her teacher she didn't wear underwear anymore just to be safe."

Something breathed on me from the right and I jumped in my seat. "Hey, Kell," Mr. Caruthers said. Somehow he and the rest of the folks at the bar had migrated around to our side and were closing in for the story.

"In school Maeve knew the answer to every question, broke boy's hearts she never even noticed and was the envy of all the rich girls. Maeve could have anything she wanted, but she was always drawn to the scoundrels, dangerous men with trouble in their eyes," Siobhan said. "In fact, her last boyfriend was so wild he would sooner chew his arm off as slip a ring on her finger."

Out of the corner of my eye I could see Mid downing a beer. Guess he gave up. Daylight streamed in once again and we all looked towards the door.

"Middleton, whatever are ya'll doing in here? We're supposed to be working," Holly's syrupy voice tinkled in the darkness.

"Shut up!" This time the chorus of voices sounded even meaner. I watched Holly and Kenneth, trailed by Kenneth's boyfriend Hans, scuttle through the angry masses and line up at the bar on the other side of Mid. Holly appeared a bit terrified. I grinned as I sipped my Bloody Mary.

"So what does her coming for a visit have to be such a problem," Mid asked.

Siobhan looked from side to side, her slanted eyes conveying a sort of helplessness.

"Don't you see, it's why the baby appeared, why Dax was murdered. It's because she's coming here, to our little island," she said. "Since her birth Maeve has turned our village in Ireland on it's head. People become, well, intoxicated around her. Brawls break out and babies appear. It's an odd mix. I believe the population has almost doubled since she came. And now she's coming here."

The roar of absolute silence literally filled the room. The air was starting to feel heavy, like clouds rolling in on a warm summer afternoon. I know Siobhan better than anyone else does, and she certainly does place a lot of belief in signs and mystery. Her sister did sound like a handful, but was she the magic potion that started this mess? For goodness sakes, she wasn't even here yet. I didn't know what was going on here, except we were all being lushes in the middle of the day.

A beer belch rumbled through the quietness. "Intoxicating, huh," Cyrus stated. "I'll drink to that."

CHAPTER TEN

I listened as the wild wind hooted and slashed outside my bedroom windows, waking me from a restless sleep where I was hounded by unanswered questions. A bolt of lighting ripped across the sky, leaving white ghostly mists floating aimlessly behind. Even from across the street I could feel the sea rising up and snarling at me.

My sheets were in a bunched up knot at the foot of my bed, probably from tossing and turning all night. Even Fred had given up and hightailed it to his own doggy bed sometime during the night to escape my agitated limbs. When the thunder cracked again it sounded like it was at my door. I grabbed my sheets and snuggled back under them.

The rain was relentless. Fine with me, I hadn't planned on running today anyways. At least we were past hurricane season. When I'd first moved here I learned that if you live in a low-lying area you best prepare yourself for evacuation. How did one determine if one was in a low-lying area? Look at your driver's license. If it says South Carolina, you live in a low lying area.

Another streak of lightening boomed. My first hurricane season here the weather people annoyed me to no end. I'd turn on the television and watch as they pointed to some radar blob out in the Atlantic and make two meteorological points; there was no need to panic and we could all be killed. Then there would be a reporter in a rain slick standing right next to the ocean telling you over and over again how vitally important it is to stay away from the ocean.

I rolled over and looked at the clock, which reflected a very respectable six a.m., not too early but my eyes still felt bleary. Yesterday had been a long day. By the time Siobhan relayed all the details regarding her sister nobody at The Coast was feeling any pain, all my dear co-workers included. Our little party came to a screeching halt when our editor flung open the door and stood like the devil himself assessing the situation. When Alex shrieked where is my staff at the top of her lungs we all pretty much stumbled our way back to the paper.

Siobhan was lucky she had already shot all the film she needed for the article. We stuck her in a chair in the corner of the news-room and got busy. First we ordered a pizza from Fat Harry's to soak up some of the alcohol. Then Myra poured coffee and made sure we all drank it. Black. A few hours later the combined article was complete. We actually did quite a good job working together, probably because the drinking had taken the edge off enough and we didn't feel like killing each other. So all in all, the day worked out. But during the night the reality of what had happened to Dax Delaray sunk in and kept me awake.

Siobhan's ramblings were nothing new, I was used to her somewhat eccentric way of thinking. Did the mysterious Maeve have anything to do with the chaos in my tiny town? I rolled over on to my stomach. The idea seemed highly unlikely as she was safe and sound on the other side of the north Atlantic ocean. For now. I forgot when Siobhan said her sister was arriving.

Who killed Dax Delaray? I'm certainly no expert when it comes to shooting somebody, but a bullet to the brain seemed sort of personal. Like if you were aiming at their head you really must not like them at all. And why hurt poor Miss Betty and Tusk? By all appearances they had simply been in the wrong place at the wrong time, but was that all it was? I flipped back over on to my back and reached for my cell phone.

"Uhglo," was how Mid answered but at least he answered.

"Mid, it's me, listen I've been thinking about the murder and all and was wondering what you make of it so far," I said. "You know, since you're the crime reporter and all."

Silence. "Mid?" I strained to hear and could make out what sounded like snoring.

"Middleton," I yelled, sitting up in bed. "Answer me!"

Something crashed on the other end of the line, and then came a spew of rather colorful words for this early in the morning. I winced and held the phone away from my ear.

"Um, Mid? Are you awake? Because I really want to talk to you….."

"Please tell me this is an emergency, Kell, because if it's not I'm going to kill you," Mid responded in a kind of creepily calm voice.

I took a deep breath and ignored him. Really, his choice of words was a bit insensitive considering the situation but I figured he wasn't in the mood to argue my point.

"Well, yes, good morning and all, I really thought you'd be up by now," I said, glancing at my clock. "It's well after six and I have this theory about how to find the killer. See, if Dax is the father of that baby, then we just have to find the mother. I really think that's the logical place to start."

I waited for Mid to agree with me, because it was honestly a great idea. Where else to look than the other person who created the child? I counted to ten and was about to shout at Middleton again when the snoring continued.

I hopped out of bed and started pacing the room. "Really, Mid, this is ridiculous, wake up! We have a killer out there! I need to talk to you about this, do you want to meet for breakfast?"

When it became obvious I was talking to myself I hung up and tossed my phone on my bed. "How can anybody sleep with this going on," I shouted. Somebody banged on my ceiling from upstairs. Fred moaned from his doggy bed and put his paws over his ears.

I took a couple of the deep cleansing breathes Siobhan preached about from yoga. I really don't like yoga much, the twisted positions seem like too much effort and I don't see the point of it all. Breathe in, breathe out. The breathing part was sort of cool, though. At least it kept me from shouting some more.

The lightning cracked the skies apart and I counted the seconds until the thunder followed. Maybe the rain would imprison me for days and I could come out when this whole mess was solved. By someone other than me.

I made a cup of coffee and wrapped my worn out purple fluffy robe around me, pulling it tight. There was no exercising today, not in this weather, so I slipped outside on to my back porch. The upstairs deck sheltered me from the rain, and I sunk in to a weathered Adirondack style chair. The sun should have been up by now, but the gloom of the morning kept it hidden. My beautiful flowers were all attempting to greet me with their array of colors. Through the mist sprung a dazzling white flower from the hostas safe in their shady corner, but that's about all I could see. The more muted shades of babies breath, trailing ivy and lime green potato vines were barely visible.

My theory was right, I was sure of it. Find the baby's mommy, find the killer. I pulled up Lurleen Higgenbottom's number from my cell phone address book. If I've ever interviewed you, you're in here.

"Hello," answered a weary voice.

"Lurleen? Kell Palevac here. I hope I didn't phone too early," I said.

Over the airwaves I heard the keening wail of what I deduced to be the infant. Through the roaring din Lurleen breathed one word I could make out. "Baby…" "Yes, the baby, that's why I'm calling, do you know how old the child is by chance?"

Lurleen must have walked in to another room because all was quiet when she spoke. "Sorry, Kell, the baby is crying, I have to be quick. How old? The pediatrician who examined her says about one month at the most. Why?"

"Um, well, it's for a story," I lied. "Hey, do you know if Bonnie has been told yet."

"Bonnie," Lurleen snorted. "Yes, she and the Mayor stopped by late last night. Woman took one look at the baby and fainted on the spot. When she came to all she could say was those are Dax's ears, eyes, you name it."

Never in my life have I seen Bonnie McLeod in a weak state, let alone fainting. She must be taking Dax's death harder than I thought.

"I offered to let her take the child but she backed off and hauled out of here so fast my head spun," Lurleen continued. "Screaming some rather horrible nonsense about her worthless brother. I believe the Mayor was going to sedate her."

Okay, so Bonnie's feelings towards Dax hadn't changed just because he was, well, dead. I said my goodbyes to Lurleen, walked inside and retrieved the phone book. I refilled my coffee and added extra cream, then plopped back down on the porch.

After a bit of searching I landed on the number for labor and delivery at a downtown hospital. A harried yet official sounding voice answered.

"Hello, I have a small problem I was hoping you could help me with," I began.

"Yes," questioned the voice.

"You see, I have this baby and we know who the father is but can't seem to find the mother. This is a Caucasian female, approximately one month old and….."

"You're kidding me, right? And just how am I supposed to help you," interrupted the voice, now a bit hostile sounding.

"Well, I was hoping we could go over the records of all females born there about one month ago and that way….."

"Listen, lady, unless you're with the police we can't release any information," replied the now impatient voice. "I have babies to attend to."

Well, for heaven's sake, she didn't need to be so testy. "Wait, wait! So I can come with the police and we can talk then?"

"Oh, sure, sweetheart, we'll have ourselves a nice little chat. Good-bye."

Geeze, nobody wanted to talk to me today. Undaunted, I dialed every hospital in town and was given the same response. One sort of nice person suggested I try the midwives and even said some women give birth at home.

"Great, so you can spit a kid out just about anywhere these days," I muttered.

"You can't spit at other kids, Kell," said a voice from above. "I got suspended from school for doing that."

I sighed heavily and looked up at the eye peering down at me. "Good morning, Elbie."

"So what're you doin' today, Kell? My mom says you've been too loud lately," Elbie said.

I stood up and finished my coffee. "Tell her sorry."

"Wait, where're you going? I want to come," Elbie whined.

A bolt of lightening lit up my back porch momentarily. I tightened my robe around me.

"I'm taking a personal day, then I've got to go to the council meeting tonight, so bye," I said, retreating back inside. Elbie was still talking but he'd finally figure out I was gone.

I crawled back in bed with my cell phone. Fred hoisted his way on to the other side and Sampson curled up at my feet. While the lightning cracked the skies apart I tuned my ears to catch the whispers on the wind, hoping for a clue.

CHAPTER ELEVEN

The few phone calls I had to make for work today took place from my bed, none too interesting except for my conversation with Bonnie McLeod. I had considered driving over to see her in person but the weather was atrocious. When I finally reached her cell phone, Mayor McLeod answered.

"She's rather delirious, Kell, so consider yourself forewarned," he said rather ominously.

Bonnie's voice sounded fine to me. "Kell, I'm so sorry I missed our meeting but you will be coming to the council meeting tonight? You can catch up on everything then, and I can hardly wait," she said excitedly.

So do I say anything about her brother or not? "Bonnie, look, I am so sorry about your brother," I said.

"What? Who? I have no idea what you're talking about," Bonnie said, her voice now starting to sound a bit shaky. "Dax was barely a brother to me, so let's not get all sappy here."

Okay, so maybe not. Too late. "Alright, I was just saying......."

"No more! Hardly a brother, and now they want to pin a baby on me! Me! Do I look like I want to be an aunt," Bonnie shrieked.

"Kell, that will be enough, you're upsetting my wife," the Mayor's voice took over. "We will see you this evening."

I reflected on the conversation while I cleaned my house. I wiped all the blinds down with soapy water and dusted away any signs of dirt. The lemon oil I use on my oak-planked coffee table made the air smell heavenly, and I vacuumed until I was positive all evidence of fur was gone.

"Show me your hooters," screeched Blackbeard. This time I did turn my can of dusting spray on him and gave him a quick blast to the feathers.

"Off with your head! Off with your head," the bird shrieked, dancing about excitedly. Well, this was a new phrase.

"I believe you're mixing up your time periods, bird. Off with your head sounds like something out of merry old England, try walk the plank," I retorted. Fred and Sampson were circling Blackbeard's cage, showing teeth and claws.

No matter what I did to stay busy while the wind whistled outside could keep my mind off my most recent dead body. Yep, I could definitely add finder of dead people to my resume. I sighed, retreated to my tranquil bathroom and submerged myself in the tub.

After allowing the conditioner in my hair to remain in place for the time required to assure I wasn't going to be a frizzy mess, I dunked under the water to rinse it out. Why do people have to take bullets to the forehead, I wondered as I emerged. The last time I had to stare at a dead girl with just such an unfortunate injury had been quite enough, thank-you very much.

The day slipped away from me and before I knew it the council meeting was just an hour away. I took a little extra time controlling my unruly hair with some sort of smoothing serum. Next was the face. After a bit of painting, blending and curling it looked like I had completed my war paint. To face town council.

Although the meeting was a still a little while from now, I decided to head there early. Someone had to have some answers about Dax by now.

I parked my car near City Hall and made my way to the meeting room. Nobody was here yet so I got a front row seat and saved the one next to me for Siobhan. After a few minutes some of the seats behind me began to fill up.

"In fact, I wouldn't mind finding the bastard myself and showing him some good ol' Folly revenge," said a gruff voice.

Several others joined in and repeated the vague threat. "Wait a minute, we can't just find Dax's killer and judge for ourselves," said one.

"Nobody tells us what to do on our island! Folly Beach is quite capable of kicking some ass if the need arises!"

I turned around. Several of the seats were occupied by folks I knew, some well and some not so well. All were longtime residents of Folly and apparently didn't like having a killer around again.

After a minute I noticed nobody was talking anymore. In fact, they were all staring. At me.

"Why, hi ya'll, good to see you," I greeted the assembling group. Nobody said a word, except for Scary Harry, who hefted a tattooed forearm in my general direction.

I cleared my throat. "So, anybody have any ideas on who killed Dax Delaray," I asked. I had my notebook out and my pen was poised just in case.

"You! You're the one who keeps finding dead people on our island," accused elderly Mrs. Pierce, pointing at me with a trembling finger.

"Hold on there, Kell hasn't done anything wrong," spoke up Beau Ashley, the owner of Beau's Barbecue Joint. He shook his head of white shaggy hair. "Listen to us, we sound like monsters."

By now most of the seats were filling up and I eves dropped on as many conversations as I could, scribbling things that caught my attention in my notebook. I felt a warm breath on the back of my neck.

"Well, well, what are you writing there, Mz. Palevac," asked Judge Preston Brooks, leaning over my shoulder. "The little reporter solved the last murder mystery we had here, maybe she'll do it again."

The uneasiness, without a name, returned as I found myself face to face with the judge. We'd always had issues with each other. I didn't like that he wanted to turn this island in to a full blown tourist attraction. Well, that and the fact that being an authority figure he could get me in trouble. He didn't like me because I'd embarrassed him in his own court room one time. Or maybe two. I forgot. The feeling I had now was different, though, vaguer and more chilling.

'Excuse me there, Judge Brooks," Siobhan said, insinuating herself between the two of us. "Just going to take my seat, why don't you go find one of your own."

Judge Brooks straightened himself up to his full height of about five feet something, his face a contorted shade of red and his beady eyes piercing me. I shuddered.

"Keep up the good work, Mz. Palevac," he hissed, moving off.

"Is it my imagination or did the good judge just hiss," Siobhan asked, shrugging off her two oversized camera bags.

"He hissed," I agreed.

"Man reminds me of a snake," Siobhan continued. "A rather short snake, maybe a lizard?"

"Definitely a lizard," I said, watching as the Mayor and council members arrived and took their seats in front of us at the long table. Mayor McLeod sat in the middle, flanked by three members on either side.

Hiram Pettigrew grabbed the gavel and began banging in an attempt to bring the meeting to order. He recently celebrated his eighty-ninth birthday and I guess Mayor McLeod lets Hiram handle the gavel due to his seniority.

Earl Jenkins leaned across Hiram. "Why does he always get the gavel," Earl asked the Mayor.

"What? I can't hear anything but this damn gavel," grumbled the Mayor.

"Quiet down, everyone, quiet down," shouted Hiram, banging the gavel a little harder.

"I'm about sick of this, Hiram. Wear your hearing aids," yelled Big Legare, grabbing the gavel.

"Help! Help," shouted Hiram, trying to wrestle the gavel back from Big, who weighs around 300 pounds and used to wrestle for a living. It wasn't much of a match.

"Elder abuse," screamed Mrs. Pierce from her seat somewhere behind me.

"Oh, for god's sake, will everyone just shut up," hollered Mayor McLeod. I noticed Big had hidden the gavel rather inventively. He sat on it.

"Well, there goes the gavel," Siobhan whispered.

"Yep, no way that thing survived," I whispered back.

Mayor McLeod announced, "The main item on the agenda for this evening's meeting is…….."

He was interrupted by the door opening. The Mayor hates tardiness. We all turned to see who would dare enter after a council meeting had begun.

CHAPTER TWELVE

I recognized Bonnie even though she had some sort of really strange contraption strapped to her face. I also recognized one of her many dogs even though he also had a strange contraption strapped to his face. His eyes met mine and I could sense the humiliation.

Bonnie was trailed by three other women who had three other dogs on leashes. All parties involved had on the same face gear. They stood in a line in front of the council members, facing us. Behind them I caught a glimpse of Mayor McLeod rising to his feet.

"Uh oh," whispered Siobhan.

"Yep," I agreed.

"Bonnie, what in the hell is going on," roared the Mayor.

Behind me I could make out similar comments. "They look like aliens," muttered someone. "Is this a joke?" People were beginning to get restless and Bonnie finally spoke.

"Okay, people, I decided a bit of shock value was in order after my last request was voted down," she began. Her voice sounded like a soft ghost-thing coming from a distance. She went on, blithely ignoring the murmurs sweeping the room.

"We," she gestured to the women standing with her. "Are wearing human oxygen masks. Our fire department has these on hand to deliver oxygen to us when we are rescued from a fire."

The hound dog wearing a mask began to howl but managed to sound like a deranged poodle. He shook his head and the lady holding his leash gave a little tug.

"These dogs are wearing pet oxygen masks, which are imperative when rescuing an animal from a fire," Bonnie continued. "A human mask on the snout of a dog does not work, and it's even worse on the snout of a cat."

"Snout of a cat? Is there such a thing," Siobhan whispered to me. I shrugged my shoulders.

"Over 40,000 animals perish from smoke inhalation each year. It's time to make our fire department top notch, so these animal masks are critical! Vote yes for pet oxygen mask funding!" With that Bonnie and her entourage exited through the doorway.

The assembled crowd behind me quickly began zealous discussions on the mask issue.

"We want masks for our animals," shouted Erma who owns the liquor store. She has a pet skunk, but I suppose a cat mask would fit the creature if need be.

"Save us from fire!"

"We demand equal equality for our pets!"

Right about when Scary Harry yelled, "Save the whales" Mayor McLeod stood up and shouted, "Silence!"

"What was that, Mayor," shouted Hiram.

"Shut up, Hiram, and the rest of you idiots! I apologize for my wife arriving unannounced, she has been under a bit of a strain recently. We will take up this issue at the next meeting, when it is officially on the agenda," the Mayor said, his face blotched with red spots.

"Excuse me, Mayor? Before we begin, we all want to express our condolences in reference to your brother-in-law," spoke up Joe Chrysalis, the owner of Mr. Joe's Beach Store. Several voices chimed in to agree with him.

Mayor McLeod waved his hand rather wearily in a dismissive motion. "Ah, well, thanks ya'll, but what I really want to know is who killed the bastard. If any of you have any clues you can call," he paused. "Her."

I turned around. Nope, he was pointing at me. "Me," I asked.

"He's pointing at you," Siobhan whispered.

"No shit," I muttered.

"Of course the Chief will want your help as well," the Mayor continued. "But in my opinion Kell Palevac is the person to go to with any information."

Well, this was nice. I sat up straight in my chair and tried to look competent.

"Yeah, well she is the one finding all the dead people around here," someone remarked behind me.

"Sure is strange, maybe she's the killer Mayor McLeod!"

"How well do we really know this lady?"

"Yeah, maybe she should be investigated!"

Siobhan leaned over to me. "Right about now is where they draw and quarter you. I here it's awfully painful, being pulled every which way like that."

"Maybe they'll be quick about it and just stick my head on a stake and march it around the island," I grumbled.

The doors flung open once again and for the second time we all turned to see what was going on. Officer Ted Adams entered the room followed by three middle aged men in hand shackles. I figured they were prisoners. Officer Clyde Bresseau brought up the rear, with Bonnie on his heals.

"Sorry, Mayor, our jail cells are full and the Chief agreed to let Mrs. McLeod bring these men here for trial," said Officer Adams.

I squinted at the three men a little closer. "It's them," I gasped.

"Them who," Siobhan asked.

"The baby raccoon killers," I stated.

"Ahh," she said.

It was a surprise to me that Bonnie hadn't executed these guys yet all by herself. Loud noises coming from the detached garage of a rental house on East Hudson woke up the next door neighbor. A local resident, the neighbor went to investigate the source of all the commotion. And discovered three very inebriated men wielding golf clubs, which they were using to wallop a family of five baby raccoons in the garage. Apparently, the fate of these three killers was about to be determined.

"Hold on a minute, I find this highly unusual," Mayor McLeod began.

"Stuff it, George, these men are mine," Bonnie shrieked at her husband. Her eyes were glassy and a bit crazed looking. Mayor McLeod rested his head in his hands.

"So, my fellow citizens of this fine island, ya'll know the story, what do we do with them," Bonnie asked, pointing at the men.

Officer Bresseau adjusted his horn-rimmed glasses and glanced up at Officer Adams.

"I think we're supposed to let the prisoners speak," he said. Adams nodded.

The first guy in line didn't waste any time. "My name is Michael Wood and I am a prominent attorney in Columbia."

Somebody tossed a crumbled up agenda meeting at him. Well, it was pretty obvious we weren't sticking to tonight's schedule anyways.

"Please help us," begged the second guy. "I'm a pediatric surgeon in Columbia and this was all a big mistake. We were a bit, um, intoxicated at the time and figured the raccoons had rabies."

Bonnie McLeod looked like a person possessed. Any minute I expected to see her head spinning around on her neck. "Enough! I propose we send them to the old jail cell for the night. If they live to see the light of day, we'll send them packing. If they don't, we'll bury them!"

The group assembled behind me let out a collective gasp. The old jail cell was basically a cage sitting in the marsh a couple blocks down. The town used it back in the 1930's or so, and I've read horrible accounts of nights spent there.

"This is not as bad as it looks. It's worse," Siobhan whispered.

The three men were looking warily from one to the other like condemned criminals.

Bonnie's laugh had a hyenalike quality to it and a smile crawled to her lips and curved itself like a snake. She then unleashed the most purple language I'd ever heard before. Pretty much. For the most part.

"To the jail cell," hollered someone. I could hear the crowd growing restless and some people began making their way to the doors. The place became a hub of confusion as folks jostled for position on their way outside.

"So, Mayor? Is this alright with you," Officer Adams asked a bit nervously.

"Ted, it would be easier to win a dog-sled race with a team of Chihuahuas than to argue with my wife right now," Mayor McLeod replied with a gusty sigh.

Within minutes the entire town council assembly was gathered at the edge of the marsh where the old iron cage sat. Officer Adams and Bresseau led the three men inside, closed the gate and padlocked it. We watched as the three prominent fixtures from Columbia realized the severity of their situation.

"Hey, hold on, where do we sit," demanded one.

"You can't leave us here, the bugs are terrible," said another, slapping his arm.

"Wait, what about snakes? Or alligators, or whatever other damned reptilians you inbreds keep on this nightmare of an island!" This last brave remark came from the unfortunate Michael Woods, Esquire.

I looked around. Inbreds? Well, technically I'm not from here, but I do consider Folly my home. I also concur completely with the locals who want outsiders to, well, stay outside. Not that we don't like tourists, we do. They at times have hysterical entertainment value and spend money quite nicely while visiting our tropical paradise. Some even come back and become islanders. Now, those born and raised on Folly are a close bunch, but inbreds? There was a rumor a few years back about Connie who works dispatch at the police station and some distant cousin, but I don't think that counts.

Something slimy skimmed my cheek and slapped me out of contemplating Mr. Wood's comment.

"Ouch," yelled the attorney.

Scary Harry and a few of the others were wading in the marsh, grabbing handfuls of pluff mud and flinging it at the old jail cell.

I spotted Cyrus and motioned for him to stop. He threw a fastball that caught one of the men smack dab in the forehead.

Complete chaos ensued, a least for a little while. It probably would have ended sooner if the officers tried to control the angry mob. Well, they did, after standing there chuckling.

Even with the commotion I could hear them.

"These people, this place, no one tells them what to do, no one has ever told them what to do," said Officer Clyde Bressau.

"Sometimes it's better to take matters in to your own hands," Officer Ted Adams replied, his barrel chest rising. "When people know justice will come quickly they behave a lot better."

I turned away from another unforgettable flaming-orange sunset streaked with a muted purple and started walking back to my car. The wind came sliding down over the world. I looked over my shoulder and could see Siobhan a few feet behind me. Near the marsh I tried to see the crowd but their figures were stolen away by the fog settling in.

CHAPTER THIRTEEN

I had my bare feet spread and braced against the outside wall of my privacy fence. The kudzu vine I was wrestling with was imbedded in my hands as I leaned back and pulled.

"Crap," I yelled, letting go of the nasty thing and falling on my rear.

"Now, Kell, my mom says to scold you when you swear," said Elbie somewhere out in the backyard.

"No, Elbie, I think she scolds you when you swear," I retorted. I hadn't finished my coffee yet and the sun was already attempting to scald away the skin on the back of my neck. "What are you doing over there?"

My gangly teenage neighbor was sitting in the grass with a bucket of water. He had a broken off piece of pampas grass in one hand and was stirring away.

"Playing with the mosquitoes," Elbie said.

"Really," I said. "Most people don't like mosquitoes."

He swatted his neck and wiped blood on his shorts. "Me neither."

"Ouch," I swatted my leg.

Elbie stopped stirring. "Look, Kell, the mosquito babies look like they're dancing in the water."

"If you dump the bucket they'll drain in to the ground and die," I suggested, swatting.

A look of horror crossed Elbie's face. "Oh, no, Kell, didn't you know they're our state bird. I couldn't kill them," he said, shaking his head.

I finished my coffee. "Actually, our state bird is the wren."

"I saw the sticker on Mayor McLeod' truck! It even has a picture of a mosquito! My teacher's wrong," Elbie jumped to his feet.

Okay, too early for Elbie. I turned to go back inside. "About what?"

"I wrote mosquito on the test as the answer! I'm right," he yelled.

"I think that sticker is supposed to be a joke," I hollered back, closing my door on the kid.

Nobody had called to say if the three prisoners had survived, so I was pretty sure they did. I took a quick shower, and did my morning routine.

"Oops, I almost forgot you, naughty bird," I stopped on my way to the front door and pulled Blackbeard's cover off.

"Off with your head!"

I leaned forward. "Where in the world did you learn that one? This is like the second time you've said it."

"Wanna have sex?"

Now that I was reassured this was indeed Blackbeard, I locked my front door on the mouthy creature.

Ludmilla was shaking out a rug off her front porch. She does this every morning, so I knew enough to scurry towards my car or get pelted with dust bunnies. Or sand. You name it. She dropped the rug and came down the side stairs with a bucket in her hands.

"Hello, Kell, off to work," Ludmilla asked, heading towards the garbage cans. I caught a glimpse of some little plastic army men, and if I was correct they appeared to be beheaded.

"What's all that," I asked.

Ludmilla sighed. "I found Elbert in his room chopping off their heads with an exacto knife."

Wow. "Um, that's weird," I said.

"He says they represent Murphy," she continued.

"Huh, Blackbeard keeps saying off with your head, maybe there's something going around," I said, smiling and waving bye.

"Funny, that is exactly why I checked on Elbert," Ludmilla stated. "He was chanting off with your head. I really do not think he cares for Murphy."

So that's where the cheeky bird learned it. Blackbeard's cage was underneath a vent that connected to Elbie's room upstairs. "Bye, Ludmilla."

As I was leaving I passed the Batmobile. I tried to duck down in my seat, which was a bit difficult since I was driving. Ugh. Murphy was just arriving. At least I left in time. Things could get bloody.

Approaching the row of oversized rocks embracing the stretch of beach known as the washout, I slowed a bit to watch the surfers. My last encounter with surfing had been for, well, personal reasons. The director of my dreams had insisted on assaulting my nights with ghastly images of the dead surfing girls I'd encountered. Siobhan had insisted I'd better surf to get them out of my head. Now, I occasionally borrowed a board from one of the local surf shops and got wet.

My hand helped shield my eyes from the blazing sun reflecting off the ocean. Whoops and war cries echoed in the air as surfers jumped effortlessly to their feet and zipped by on itty bitty pieces of fiberglass. The exhilaration must be intense. Me, I manage to paddle out and not get in anybody's way. Too much. I recognized Beau's daughter Cristina mostly because of her itty bitty polka dot bikini.

My cell phone rang and reminded me I was on my way to work. I picked up the pace.

"Kell here."

" Hello?"

"Yes, this is Kell, who is this?"

"Yes, this is Erma, from the liquor store," came the reply.

Everyone knows who Erma is but she acts like she is not aware of this. I guess it's because she doesn't want to seem too friendly with her customers. Come to think of it, those brown paper bags do provide a lot of anonymynity. Must be part of the business.

"Hey, Erma" I said, swerving around a bicyclist.

"I have a theory," Erma said.

Okay, story idea? I listened.

"I have a list of suspects for you, just stop by the store," she whispered.

"Huh?"

"We got your number from the Mayor. So we could let you know our theories. We have ideas about the murderer," Erma was trying to whisper but sort of squeaked.

Wonderful. He gave out my number to, well, whoever we meant. I was assuming the entire island. Maybe Erma spoke in the third person.

"Sure, Erma, I'll swing by sometime," I replied. "Uh, thanks."

"You're quite welcome," Erma said and disconnected.

By the time I reached Center Street there were three more similar calls from locals. When the phone rang again I let it go to voice mail. It rang once more as I pulled in to the one and only gas station on Folly.

"Geeze, I guess I need to find out the current population around here," I grumbled, getting out. "Then I'll know how many more times that thing's going to ring."

The crumbled ten dollar bill was still in my jeans pocket where I'd stuck it the night before.

"Here you go, Brandy," I said, handing it to the cashier. "Pump three."

"Sure," Brandy said, pushing her rather cute green glasses up on her perky nose. "Are you coming to the sacrifice tonight?"

For crying out loud, this better not have anything to do with the prominent guys from Columbia.

"What sacrifice," I asked cautiously.

Behind the cute glasses Brandy's eyes narrowed rather ominously. Her perky little nose wrinkled. "My ex-husband's."

I raised my eyebrows. "Ronald? You're sacrificing Ronald? Really, Brandy, that doesn't sound like a great idea," I said. "Not to mention probably illegal."

"Not Ronald. Ronald's surfboards, all five of them," she spat. "Bastard left me when things got tight. When the money was around, so was he."

"Whew, well, that does sound a bit better than Ronald himself," I conceded. "So, how do you sacrifice surfboards?"

"Meet us at the washout at 8 p.m. Dead low-tide and the waves are slamming. I'm letting all volunteers ride the boards straight in till they snap in half," Brandy said with her folded across her chest. "Have loads of volunteers."

I turned to leave. "Good luck with all that."

"Oh, Kell," Brandy exclaimed. "I almost forgot. Ronald could be the killer. Heard the Mayor said to tell you our ideas."

I paused. "What?"

"Yeah, he's such a bastard I could totally see him doing it," she said.

"Concentrate on the sacrifice, Brandy," I said. "We all know Ronald's an idiot, but a killer? Doesn't have the balls."

Brandy brightened considerably. "Yeah, that's what I thought. It was just an idea."

I hit the dip in the exit on my way out of the gas station with an extra wallop, then swung a quick left and headed to work. Okay, so I drive too fast, and thinking about money irritates me to no end. Poor Brandy. Come to think of it, poor me. Shouldn't I be getting a raise after all these years?

Siobhan was sitting in the chair across from my desk with her feet up. I sighed and left them alone.

"What's up," I asked.

"Me? Waiting for a moment to go ask helmet head for a raise," Siobhan replied, stretching her long arms above her head. "Got some fantastic shots of the incarcerated men. And did I tell you about the sacrifice tonight at the washout?"

"Just saw Brandy," I replied, swinging my black bag with all my gear in it on to my desk. "A raise? That's what I was thinking, are you reading my thoughts?"

"Possibly," Siobhan said. She was twirling a long strand of reddish hair around her finger. "Maeve's imminent arrival is creating a myriad of mystifying events."

I sighed. "Okay."

"You better think up a good one asking Alex for a raise," she recommended. "I've got mine down."

This was rather sudden. I hadn't thought of a story. "Any ideas," I asked.

"Try the Poe angle," she said over her shoulder as she walked to Alex's office.

"The what?"

"First person to earn a living as a writer, a pitiful amount at that from what I've heard," Siobhan said. "Look how he turned out."

CHAPTER FOURTEEN

I scurried after her. No way was she getting a raise and I wasn't.

"Hold up, what should I say about Poe," I asked.

Siobhan stopped and wrinkled her nose. "Well, just tell Alex how Poe is one of your inspirations but you shudder at the fact that writers still don't earn enough."

Sounded good to me. "Why, exactly, do I shudder," I asked.

Her green eyes glittered. "Because Edgar has probably turned over hundreds of times in his grave by now. He's horrified that no progress has been made. He was a very poor man, you know. Come on," Siobhan said, grabbing my arm.

Alex DeWinter was sitting behind her desk inside the glass enclosure whe calls an office. The whole thing is just walls of glass, which is exactly how she planned it. This way she can keep an eye on all of us.

"I didn't realize you were bringing Kell along," Alex said. "I only have a minute."

Before I could even say hello Siobhan launched in to a monologue detailing why she deserved a raise and ended it quite nicely by suggesting she was courted by other publications. Alex narrowed her icy blue eyes and shook her head, which didn't affect her hair one bit.

"Really, Siobhan, you didn't need to go to all the trouble with that lovely speech," she said. "Mr. Lyons already approved your request."

Siobhan looked surprised, but recovered quickly. "I'll be sure to thank our publisher."

"You do that. Now, what do you want, Kell," Alex asked, shifting her focus to me.

I cleared my throat. "Yes, well, I was thinking I could use a raise as well."

Alex just stared at me without blinking.

"So, you see, writers in general don't earn enough, and this dates back to the days of Edgar Allen Poe," I continued. "He was forced to make humiliating pleas for money during his literary career."

Alex didn't reply.

I shifted uncomfortably in my seat. "Sort of like I'm doing right now," I muttered.

My editor rose slowly to her feet behind her desk. "I had no idea you were such a Poe fan, Kell," she said. "I absolutely adore Edgar!

Do you know they lied about him after his unfortunate death? His arch enemy Rufus Griswold tried to destroy his reputation!"

Siobhan looked at me with a grin. I'd never seen Alex DeWinter so animated. There was even a little color coming to her usually milky white complexion. She began pacing around her office.

"Do you know Griswold portrayed Edgar as a depraved, drunk, drug-addled madman? Why, the stories I can tell you about poor Edgar," Alex exclaimed brightly.

By the time we staggered out of her office I knew more than I wanted to about the effects of decomposition, premature burial and the reanimation of the dead. Now I remembered why I didn't much care for the class I took on Poe in college.

I flopped down in my chair and Siobhan perched on the edge of my desk, whistling some sort of Irish melody. "That went well. Now I know why Alex has always reminded me of a vampire. She's in love with Edgar," she said.

"Well? You get a raise and I get a lecture about how happy I should be to follow in Poe's footsteps," I grumbled. "Maybe I should switch careers now before they find me delirious in the streets."

Holly stopped typing at her desk across from me. "What was that, Kell? Did you say you're switching careers? So you'll be leaving," she asked a bit too cheerfully.

I stared her down. "No, Holly, I intend to stay. Forever."

"Say, Holly, I see you covered the story about that new cupcake bakery place downtown," Siobhan interjected.

Holly raised her arched eyebrows. "Why, how did you know that, I'm just working on the article now."

Siobhan tilted her head to the side and squinted in Holly's direction. "Anyone can see you got to sample all the cupcakes. They really turn straight to fat in a hurry."

"Why, I never! You are so mean, both of you," Holly shrieked, jumping to her feet and scurrying off towards the bathrooms.

Siobhan and I high-fived each other. "Good one," I said.

"Great, you guys," said Kenneth from his desk. "Now she'll be asking me how she looks for weeks."

"Make sure to tell her the cupcakes are showing," Siobhan suggested. "Listen, I'm out. Have to go get some shots of the Calhoun place as it's being decorated for tonight."

Uh oh. What was I forgetting? If Mid's parents house was being decorated there had to be something important going on. Their mansion downtown was the site of many festivities, most of which I was expected to attend as either a reporter of friend. Or both. I searched my brain.

"Okay, I give up," I hollered at Siobhan as she was making her exit. "Decorated for what exactly?"

Siobhan gave me one of her innocent smiles. "Remember like a month ago? When Mid told us about the big party for his mom's birthday?"

I groaned and put my head down on my desk.

"Remember I began bugging you about what you were going to wear," she continued. "And I quote, bugging you."

I waved a hand at her, trying to shoo her out the door.

"So I figured you could handle it. You should see my dress, it's dreamy," Siobhan said. "See you tonight!"

Maybe I could just keep my head on my desk and sleep through the party. Shit. My clothes selection consists of jeans, t-shirts, shorts and of course, some really cute running gear. I did have like two dresses to my name, but I've worn them both so many times. Maybe I had accessories.

I was creating all sorts of reasons to explain my absence from tonight's festivities, none of which included nothing to wear, when Holly stopped by my desk on her return from sulking in the bathroom. I knew this because with my head down I could see the stupid shoes she was wearing parked in my space.

"What do you want," I asked without raising my head.

Holly tapped her left foot. "Me? Oh, nothing, just on my way to the spa. I have a massage, pedicure, manicure and blow-out scheduled. I simply cannot wait for the party tonight!"

I peaked at my nails. Maybe I could do them myself. I totally understand the massage, mani and pedi part, but who has to pay someone just to blow dry their hair?

"Well, I'm off," Holly continued. "I have to get ready."

When I was sure she was gone I jumped out of my chair and grabbed my bag. Somewhere in there my cell phone was ringing.

I dug it out and saw I'd missed eighteen calls. Great. The whole island had leads to Dax's murder, so I guess I had some calls to return.

"Not now," I muttered to myself. "Now I have to go find something to wear." No way was Holly going to the party and I wasn't.

Myra Glass was watering the peace lilies near her desk as I was making my exit. There are about seven of them in various planters, and I think she keeps them to ward off all the angry vibrations in the office. Well, for crying out loud, Holly causes all the tension around here.

"Kell, dear, wait until you see my dress tonight," Myra said. "It's quite elegant."

I paused. It's also probably beige, the only color the woman wears is on the chain attached to her glasses.

"Let me guess, Myra. It's beige," I said a bit sarcastically.

She put a hand to her chest. "Why, yes, although the saleswoman called it champagne."

I bit my tongue. No need to get testy with poor Myra, it certainly wasn't her fault I had nothing to wear. Squaring my shoulders, I stood tall, brave and determined to venture out where I hardly ever go. Shopping.

"I'm sure it's beautiful," I said on my way out the door. "Bye."

CHAPTER FIFTEEN

A few hours later I was standing in front of the full length mirror on my door. Shopping had been painful, but the results were worth it.

"Beautiful," I whispered to the dress in the mirror.

"Woof," barked Fred in agreement.

I twirled a bit and the dress twirled with me. The saleswoman had called it silk charmeuse jacquard. I called it a heavenly shade of pale green with polka dots in the pattern.

Siobhan and I usually ride together but tonight I was on my own. I had taken extra time getting ready and kept checking my face in the rear view mirror. Well, until I sort of swerved and some impatient driver blasted their horn.

By keeping my eyes on the road I managed to make it in one piece to the historical mansion downtown where Mid grew up. The place was lit up like a Christmas tree. I took a deep breath and made my way inside.

Usually I have Siobhan with me at these events, but for some reason she wasn't here yet, so I wandered around alone. The small talk was getting boring and the champagne the nice waiters kept plying me with was going straight to my head. My cell phone was tucked inside the little black clutch I brought, and the thing rang so often I wanted to shoot it. All these leads to Dax's murder weren't going to bother me tonight.

"Why, Kell, darlin', there you are! Look, Middleton, Kell is here," trilled Ella Kay, the guest of honor, kissing my cheek. "You look absolutely gorgeous!"

"I concur," Mid said with a slight bow of his head.

I grabbed another glass of champagne from a passing waiter and twirled in my new dress. "Well, I sort of splurged. Do you like it?"

Mid offered me a hand so I twirled again. "Kell," he said solemnly. "Stunning."

I was giggling from the champagne bubbles and finally having a bit of fun chatting with the two of them when a familiar syrupy voice spoiled it all.

"Cute polka dots, Kell," Holly drawled.

I turned around. Holly was squeezed in to some sort of gold, glittery floor length gown with a plunging neckline. Somehow she always gets her hair exactly right, all shiny auburn ringlets piled high on top of her head. She batted what had to be false eyelashes at me and dug her glossy red nails in to the arm she was holding.

"Uh, cute nails, Holly," I managed.

She smirked and batted a bit more. "Oh, look who's back in town," she said, gesturing to the arm she was clinging to. I looked up.

"Kelll. It's been too long," the arm extended itself and offered a hand.

The durably boyish face had matured over the years, the planes a little more angular. The blonde hair had darkened a bit, but the full lips set in a perpetual sneer were still the same. His pale blue eyes slid over me.

"Gosh, Charles, I haven't seen you since college," I said, rather surprised, shaking his hand.

Charles Heyward had been Holly's boyfriend back when we all were at the College of Charleston together, and had also pursued me relentlessly. He held my hand and gently kissed the top. His arm went back around Holly's waist and I swear she purred.

"Charles just got back," she said with a toss of her head. The ringlets practically jingled.

"Huh, you don't say," I said, reaching inside my bag to silence the ring of my cell phone. Again. "Back from where, Charles?"

He held Holly close to his side. I was hoping she'd pop. "Oh, me? I've been out of the country, over in England as a matter of fact," Charles responded. "What's up with that phone there, Kell? Maybe you should switch it off, this is a party, after all."

The arm around Holly had slid up so it was now caressing her shoulder. She looked so damn pleased with herself, although personally I'd never considered Charles much of a catch.

"Oh, haven't you heard, you dear boy," Holly giggled. "Kell is in charge of finding the latest killer we have on Folly. It's her specialty now, dead bodies. So ladylike."

"Shut up, Holly, I'm not in charge of anything," I retorted, silencing my ringing phone once again. Maybe Charles had a point. I switched it to silent. "What were you doing over in England?"

A passing waiter paused long enough for us all to grab more champagne. Charles downed his and motioned for another. "Me? Yeah, well, I've been there a year or so now, had a relationship that recently ended," he said. "But enough about me. What is this you've got going on, Kell?"

The arm had now worked it's way to my waist and guided me away. I looked over my shoulder and I'm pretty sure I saw Holly snarl.

"It's silly, really, there was a murder on Folly and for some reason the Mayor decided to field all calls to me," I said. "Personally, I think it's because he doesn't want to deal with everybody."

"Calls? So that's why your phone rings constantly," Charles said, smiling. "I was hoping it wasn't all your admirers, although I'm sure there are many." He took a healthy swig of champagne.

"No such luck," I chuckled.

Holly had started to slide towards us and Charles took my elbow and led me to the next room. "So, do you have any idea about who the killer is?"

"Honestly, no, I really haven't had time to sort through the leads yet. It's the strangest thing, but, hey, this is a party. Enough business talk," I declared.

Charles was staring at me with such deadly concentration I was sure I had something stuck in my teeth. He held his head back arrogantly as though sniffing something. "Hey, sorry I asked, just trying to see what you've been up to."

Great, now I'd insulted him. "Really, let's talk about something else. Tell me about England," I said, resting my hand on his arm.

Now that I'd soothed his ego Charles was happy to entertain me with stories from across the pond. Every once in a while I could see Holy lurking in the shadows, steam coming out of her ears. When she couldn't stand it anymore she descended upon us with forced gaiety and theatrical bitchiness.

"Why, I declare, Kell, you've been hogging Charles to yourself all evening," she simpered. "Time to give him up."

"No problem, I really should mingle," I said. "Where on earth is Siobhan?" It wasn't like her to miss a party.

Charles was staring at me with such intensity it brought a bit more color to his eyes. "Stay, Kell," he insisted, shrugging off Holly's arm. "Let's talk a bit more." The coaxing timbre of his voice reminded me of days gone by when he tried dating me in college. I felt a momentary twinge of exasperation.

"It's been great catching up," I said, keeping my tone neutral. "I'm going to go search for Siobhan, you're in quite capable hands here, Charles."

Holly's voice had a sweet edge to it, kind of like sugar spun into icicles. "He most certainly is. Hurry on, Kell, go search for your friend," she said, digging her nails in to Charles's jacket. His face radiated a sort of controlled anger, and I made my escape before anything happened. Last time Holly thought I was interested in Charles I ended up slugging her.

Kenneth Linksi and his German better half, Hans, were across the room so I decided to go chat with them for a bit. Maybe they knew were Siobhan was.

"Linski, Hans," I greeted them. "You both look quite handsome tonight."

"Well, thanks, Kell, you look gorgeous," Linski said. Hans merely grunted. "Looks like Charles Heyward agrees."

I peeked over my shoulder and sure enough Charles was isolating on me while Holly fawned over him. Huh, maybe I should dress up more often. I flung my hair back with a bit more energy than usual. Maybe I could get used to this femme fatale role.

"Boys, do ya'll know where Siobhan is at, it's not like her to miss a party," I asked.

Linski yanked on his tie, which was an odd shade of mauve. Nah, haven't seen her. Fix my tie, will you Hans?"

Naturally stoic and generally self contained, Hans had a glazed- over look to his eyes and his mouth was hanging open in a rather unflattering manner.

"Hans! I said fix my tie," Linski demanded, tugging on Hans' brawny bicep.

Hans shrugged him off and slowly began moving away towards what appeared to be a group of people gathered around someone. I stood on my tip toes, which was sort of hard in high heels, but I couldn't see anything. Hans is quite tall, so I was guessing he could see what was happening.

"Hans! Where are you going," Linski shouted. He's only a couple inches taller than me and began jumping up and down. "What's going on, what do you see?"

As Hans reached the crowd the masses parted a bit and I finally found out where Siobhan was . I could hear her voice with its Irish lilt talking to the woman standing next to her, who seemed to be the center of all this attention. She had an aura of untouchable glory about her, and even from a distance I could see her beauty was so unearthly it was frightening.

I took a deep breath and grabbed Linski by the arm. "Come on, it's about time we meet Siobhan's sister."

CHAPTER SIXTEEN

First thing I noticed was Siobhan had certainly had her fair share of the champagne flowing so freely tonight. Her green eyes looked like chipped emeralds set in a web of red blood vessels. She sucked her mouth into a rosette and blew me a kiss as I got closer.

"Where have you been," I asked, giving her a quick hug.

"The Coast! Had to properly introduce my sister to Folly when she arrived, now didn't I," Siobhan said with a curiously bright smile. "Kell Palevac, my baby sister Maeve."

I studied the creature before me. Wild, exotic sapphire eyes that tilted catlike set in a heart shaped face. Her hair was a plume of black gold falling to her waist. It caught the light from the chandeliers and was illuminated with luxuriant drama. The simple black dress she was wearing molded itself to a body that was both slender and voluptuous at the same time. She wasn't as tall as Siobhan, but she held herself like a queen. I held out my hand.

"Bollocks, don't be daft, I've heard so much about you," Maeve said, drawing me close for a squeeze. "I was hoping we'd meet someday."

Her accent with it's singsong lilt was similar to Siobhan's. It was a night voice, though, not a morning one, like dark liquid mixed with velvet. For a moment my thoughts were like gliding clouds, fading in and out of the heavens. I could hear the tinkle of ice cubes in someone's drink and the whisper of voices around me. I removed myself from Maeve's embrace and shook my head.

"Welcome to the States," I greeted her. "First time here?"

Someone was breathing down my neck. Hans still had his mouth open like a bass caught on a line. Matter of fact, it appeared the whole party was drawn together to gaze at the apparition in our midst. I elbowed Hans out of the way a little and looked at Siobhan.

"Like moths to a flame, told you so," she whispered in my ear.

"Quit telling secrets," Siobhan scolded her sister. "Actually, Kell, this is my first time away from home. I'd never been keen on traveling before, but I felt drawn to your little Folly Beach island."

"Told you," Siobhan whispered again. I swatted her away.

Hans had moved closer and was leaning towards Maeve, peering into her face as though studying a painting in a museum. He wasn't the only one. All around me I felt the crowd closing in for a better look, their faces reflecting something somewhere between disbelief and enchantment. I felt something like the burst of magic bubbles in my head and then Linski's voice was loud and clear.

"What the hell? Snap out of it, Hans, she's, well, a she! What are you going to do, start batting for the other team," Linski demanded in a perturbed wail.

"For shame, Murphy," wailed Ludmilla. "Stop gobbling up the child with your eyes." She smacked Murphy upside his head. I nodded a greeting to the two of them.

Murphy focused on Maeve like a man possessed. "Hardly a child," he breathed.

My reporter's antennae picked up the subtle increase in tension right before the explosion. The refined party was suddenly a madness of emotions pushed to the limits. Voices shouted at their significant others in open hostility and Siobhan grabbed me by the arm.

"Look, this is how it is," she said. "I warned you." Her eyes had a maniacal glint to them.

"Wait a minute, I thought Maeve brought with her lovey dovey feelings, not this craziness," I said, ducking as a champagne glass flew by my head.

"First the uncontrollable jealousy and rages, then eventually they'll start mating like rabbits," Siobhan stated. "Oh, shit, Linski is taking this hard."

Linski had jumped on Hans' back. He appeared to be holding on for dear life with one hand and scratching the hell out of Hans' cheek with the other. Somewhere a fist connected with somebody's nose and a chair went sailing through the air. Through the din I spotted Charles still intently focused on me. Huh, he was the only one not affected by the vision that was Maeve. I flung my hair back.

Siobhan had Hans by the ear and was pulling him towards the front entrance with Linski still stuck to his back. "Get out of here, go on now," she ordered.

"We don't have a ride," Linski moaned. His arms were wrapped so tight around Hans' neck I was afraid he would choke him.

"Oh, for heaven's sake, come on, I'll take you," I said, grabbing Hans by the other ear. "We're out of here. Beautiful dress, by the way."

Siobhan grinned and dodged an unfortunate waiter who had been flung into the melee. "Thanks, darlin'. Call me tomorrow."

I left downtown as fast as possible and practically flew over the James Island connector. Stars sparkled like diamonds in the clear night sky, guiding me back to the refuge that was Folly Beach. Linski was sitting beside me with his arms folded across his chest. I noticed his glasses were dangling off one ear.

"Stop pouting," I instructed, reaching over and straightening them out.

"Drunk," Hans muttered from the back seat. "You're not drunk, you're German," screeched Linksi.

"Don't even try that excuse!"

"Drunk," Hans insisted.

"Listen, you can yodel drunk all you want, I'm not buying it," Linski shouted.

I'm pretty sure it's the Swiss who yodel, but Linksi looked a bit like a rabid dog so I bit my tongue.

"I think what he's talking about is the way Maeve affects people," I said, patting his hand. "Remember, Siobhan said her name means she who makes men intoxicated.

"Yah," Hans agreed.

Linski snorted. "Okay, possibly men who are interested in women. You certainly didn't see me getting all hot and bothered," he said, pulling his hair up. "We really might have to rethink our relationship, Hans."

"Nah," Hans said.

Linski had turned around in his seat. "Well, do you still find me attractive? Are you sure this is what you want, Hans? We've been together a long time, do you still find me desirable?"

"Yah," Hans said.

I massaged my forehead with one hand and dug my nails in to the steering wheel with the other.

"Listen, guys, you two are great together, let's just forget about this and go grab a beer, okay? Look, we're here," I said as the little bridge deposited us on to Folly. "So kiss and make up, or whatever it is you do."

"Yah," Hans said.

CHAPTER SEVENTEEN

Center Street was alive with the sound of locals. I gave the wheel a quick jerk to the left and maneuvered my way in to a small spot on East Hudson, barely missing the front end of a bright pink golf cart parked at an angle. The license plate on the back said Red Headed Step Child.

"Looks like Barefoot Brenda got a new ride," Linski said as we climbed out.

"Yah," Hans agreed with a burp.

A glint of metal caught my eye from across the street. "Hold up, guys," I said.

There is a wonderful mural painted on the side wall of The Folly Star, a little joint quite popular with the locals. They have a tank of hermit crabs, each painted with a different number. Every Wednesday night you can come by, pick out a crab, and participate in the hermit crab races. Winner gets to eat and drink free for the evening. I've played a couple times but my crab never wins. The mural depicts some famous people in an eerily life-size manner, and right now someone was having a shoot out with John Wayne.

"Come on," I said, grabbing Linski by the arm. "This could be difficult."

"Wait a minute, Kell, that guy's got a gun," Linski replied, trying to squirm out of my grasp. Hans grabbed him by the other arm and together we made our way towards the mural.

"Ready, set, draw!" The fellow with the gun wasn't playing. He fired off a few rounds which ricocheted off the wall.

"Ouch," yelled Linski, grabbing his knee. "I've been shot! Help, police!"

"Will you hush up," I yelled back. "They're just pellets. Elbie, what in the hell are you doing?"

Elbie turned towards us with the gun pointed at Linski, who dropped to his knees and covered his head with his arms. Hans snapped out of his drunken haze and made a grab for the gun, which really wasn't a good idea. Sure, Hans is a tall, muscular German brute, but Elbie is just as tall and has a few screws loose. Trust me, I've lived below him for a few years now.

"Let go of my gun," screamed Elbie as he wrestled Hans for the silver pistol.

"Nah," Hans hollered. "Gif me da gun!"

Pellets rained down on us as the gun went off. I glanced around to see if we were in danger of being arrested, but nobody walking the streets was paying any attention to us. Just another day in paradise. I gave Elbie a swift kick in his rear end.

"Enough already, Elbert holster that thing. Linski, get up. Move everyone, get inside." I herded the three of them through the open doors of The Folly Star. We tripped over each other and sort of plowed to a halt once inside. At least we were all standing up.

"Evening, Kell," said Carmen the waitress as she wiped down a table. "Ya'll have a seat."

"Everybody sit," I ordered through clenched teeth. My ankle twisted as I landed in my chair. I'd forgotten I had high heels on when I kicked Elbie and apparently one snapped in the process.

"Three Budweisers and a Coke," I requested.

"My mom says I'm not allowed to drink Coke," Elbie said, staring at Carmen's ample bosom. "She says it has too much sugar in it and could make me hyper. What's hyper mean anyways, Kell?"

I massaged my forehead. "Just bring him a water, Carmen."

"No way, I don't like water. Can I have a Dr. Pepper," Elbie asked.

"Fine," I said.

Carmen tilted her head to the side. "Yeah, but doesn't......."

"Just bring it," I bellowed.

"Geeze, Kell, you don't have to yell. My mom says you yell way too much, and you curse too much," Elbie said. "My mom says......."

"Can we all please just shut up," I interrupted. The night had been a fiasco, I had a headache and my shoe was broken. I kicked my heels off and felt the chill of the wooden floor on my bare feet. Maybe me and Barefoot Brenda could go hang out together. Far, far away from people. These people.

Carmen brought our drinks and I downed a serious slug. I missed my Coronas, but the Budweisers were cheaper and as it didn't appear I was getting a raised anytime soon I was trying to cut corners.

"So, Elbie, what are you doing out on Center Street so late," I asked, resting the cold can against my forehead.

Elbie was blowing bubbles in his Dr. Pepper. I took another swig. He moved his straw from his mouth to one nostril and continued blowing bubbles.

"Gross," said Linksi.

"Yah," agreed Hans.

I gulped down my beer and took away Elbie's toy.

"Stop it, Kell, give me my straw," he shouted.

"Listen, buddy, I've had just about enough for one night," I retorted. "What are you doing out here so late?"

"You already asked me that," Elbie replied sullenly.

"Right, so answer."

Elbie picked a fresh scab on his arm until it bled.

"Gross," said Linski.

"Yah," agreed Hans.

I stood up and threw some money on the table. "Ya'll can stay here and visit John Wayne out there or maybe Elvis. I'm outta here."

I flounced outside in my party dress and bare feet, followed by the Three Stooges.

"Where we goin', Kell," Elbie asked.

I tried to walk faster than everyone else but they kept up, probably because of my bare feet. I plucked my cell phone from my clutch and dialed Ludmilla. She didn't answer, so I left a message telling her to come retrieve her son.

"No way, I ain't goin' home, Murphy's there," Elbie whined.

"Fine," I said, walking faster towards the beach. People were spilling out of restaurants and the street was getting a little crowded. I kept up my pace and so did the people I seemed to be stuck with. We all maneuvered our way around a tipsy guy blocking the sidewalk and finally reached my destination.

I counted ten Harleys lined up outside The Coast. Cyrus was standing guard at the door, all dressed up in his finest biker attire. He gave me the once over and whistled his approval. I flung my hair back.

"Pretty fancy duds for this place, darlin'," Cyrus said, engulfing me in a bear hug as my three companions stood by.

"Came from Mid's parents' party," I replied.

Cyrus snorted and shook his head. "Glad I missed it," he said. Middleton is not one of his favorite people, probably because they don't have much in common. I mean, Cyrus is a biker and Mid is, well, Mid. Even irons his jeans.

I glanced inside and could make out a few faces I knew through the smokey haze. Live music spilled out in to the streets, as did a couple of serious looking biker dudes. They lit cigarettes and perched on what had to be there very own bikes. You never, ever touch a bike if it's not yours. I guess Elbie missed that memo. He was stroking the side of a beautiful silver beast with really tall handlebars.

"Elbie, don't touch," I instructed just as my cell phone rang.

"Kell here," I said.

"Yes, Kell, why on earth do you have Elbert down on Center Street at this hour," demanded Ludmilla. "It's past his bedtime."

"Look, I didn't bring him, but you need to come pick him up," I retorted, keeping an eye on the overgrown teenager. "Outside The Coast."

"The Coast! What is my child doing at that place," Ludmilla shrieked. I held the phone away from my ear.

"Elbie, stop," I shouted a moment too late. He leaned back against the bike he was admiring, arms folded with his hands behind his head and it went down. In fact, they all went down like dominoes.

Guess bikers have really good hearing because even with the live music blaring a bunch of them suddenly appeared at the door.

"Oh, shit," moaned Linski.

"Yah," agreed Hans.

"Hurry up," I shouted to Ludmilla and hung up. "A little help here!"

Cyrus moved fast and hauled Elbie to his feet. The bikers were starting to make some really scary faces and even more disturbing remarks. Cyrus flung Elbie over his shoulder, not an easy task, I might add and hurried inside The Coast, presumably to hide him in the office. At least, that's what I was hoping for.

"His mother will be here soon," I shouted to Cyrus amidst the growing crowd of biker dudes who were starting to look pretty pissed off.

"I'm leaving, Kell," Linksi hollered, clinging to Hans' brawny bicep.

For once I had nothing to argue about with Linski. I grabbed Hans' other bicep and we fled across the street towards the beach.

CHAPTER EIGHTEEN

The bright moonlight was like a lacing of crystals on the black velvet water, bringing a magical aura to the ocean. I watched as the waves lifted to the stars only to fall short and crash to the shore. I could sort of relate. Sometimes it felt like I was reaching for something practically in my grasp that was unattainable. Maybe it was time to pay attention to my leads on who killed Dax Delaray.

"Let's walk a little," I said to my two companions, retrieving my cell phone from my clutch. Our shadows lay ahead of us in a long slanted pattern against the damp sand.

Linski was hyperventilating and pulling his hair straight up so hard it was in danger of being removed from his head. "That was close, I thought we were gonna be killed," he gasped. "What's wrong with that kid, anyways? He's like a walking time bomb."

"It's complicated," I said with a sigh. "Let's listen to some of these messages." I switched on the speaker phone option and turned the volume up.

There were so many calls I lost track of them. Many were anonymous, others boldly identified themselves as having the key to the killer's identity. I knew pretty much everybody who left a message, even the ones trying to be discreet about who they were. Hey, it's a small town. Not real easy hiding around here.

"This is ridiculous," Linski said with a snort. "Does Mrs. Pierce really think nobody knows it's her blaming Hiram for all this? Aren't they a little too old to keep up this stupid fight?"

"Yah," agreed Hans.

I walked along the edge of the ocean, letting the water cover my bare feet. Apparently Hiram and Mrs. Pierce had a half-centuries old lovers' quarrel still brewing. Now that sounded like a good story idea, it was exactly the sort of stuff I like to write about. Human interest, local events, people. Sure, Hiram and Mrs. Pierce were old, but they were still alive. I picked up a shell and flung it at the ocean.

"I'm sick and tired of all these dead people and who killed who and all of it," I shouted at the sea. A rogue wave sprung up and caught me by surprise, smacking against my bare legs in response. Great, now my new dress was wet. I wrung the fabric between my hands and squeezed every last drop of saltwater out that I could.

"Chill out, Palevac. At least your boyfriend wasn't fawning over someone else," Linski said with a sniff.

"I don't have a boyfriend," I shouted again.

"Maybe need," suggested Hans.

I picked up my pace and stormed off ahead of them. Why did the Mayor have to pin this mystery on me? Just because I was sort of, okay, really wrapped up in the last murders we had on Folly didn't mean I was in charge around here. For goodness sakes, Mid was the crime reporter and last time I checked there were police around the island. I scratched at the scar on my thigh, cursing my misfortune. Then I tripped.

"Shit," I spat through a mouthful of seaweed. The pile, mixed in with a variety of shells, was so big I should have seen it. I scooted around until I was at least firmly planted on my rear end and pulled slime out of my teeth. A rare pale pink shell stuck in the mess caught my eye and I reached for it. At least I'd found a treasure to add to my collection.

I tugged the shell out of the seaweed clinging to it and four more pink shells came with it.

"Hey, Kell, you okay," Linski asked as he and Hans caught up to me. "Hans, help her up."

For a short time, probably no more than it took to take a deep breath, confusion made me feel like a child who had stumbled upon something he didn't understand. My whole body tightened and a whisper of terror ran through me as a scream clawed at the back of my throat. I dropped the shells that weren't really shells but the remnants of a pink pedicure decorating the toes of the foot in my hand. My stomach heaved and then the stars twinkled good-bye as my head hit the sand.

CHAPTER NINETEEN

Something tickled. I blindly reached with my hand and swatted at the irritation. Something was also ringing incessantly near my ear so I swatted at that, too. Nothing happened so I opened my eyes and stared at the stars. And remembered where I was.

"Shit," I screamed above the roar of the ocean, scurrying away as fast as I could from the pile of seaweed. The pink-toed foot I had held in my hand was attached to a leg now visible in the tangled kelp. A few feet away I spotted Hans and Linski. Hans appeared to be passed out in the sand and Linski was huddled next to him, spewing gibberish.

"Yep, yep, yep," he muttered. "Leg, yep, yep. Ha! Gotcha! Yep, yep, leg."

I scooted over towards them and smacked Linski upside the head. "Kenneth Linski! Snap out of it!"

"Uggh," he moaned and promptly passed out face down in the sand next to Hans. Geeze, I didn't hit him that hard. At least he was quiet, I needed a moment to think.

I snuck a peek at the pink-toed leg. The moonlight was bright enough to reveal something the size of a body tangled in the seaweed, so I deduced the leg was attached to, well, its body. No need to make sure. Common sense told me this was most likely a female, due to the pedicure and all. Now that I'd solved this little mystery I was ready to go home. Yep, all in a good day's work, I'd just meander off and leave the two, well, three of these people in the sand and head to bed.

Standing up proved harder than usual. The stars glittered mockingly, all bright and cheerful against the night sky. The ringing noise from earlier started up again and I retrieved my cell phone from the sand.

"Kell here," I methodically answered, not a care in the world, well, except for the annoying looking leg I couldn't stop staring at. Somewhere in my dazed state I decided this just wouldn't do, so I began the traipse through the sand back towards the street.

"Finally," shouted Cyrus as something crashed rather loudly. "Holy shit, Stuay, put the table down!"

I held my phone away from my ear as more smashing and crashing ensued.

"Not there, Stuay, oh, shit," Cyrus shouted again.

The sand slowed my pace a bit, but I was almost towards the street. Maybe I should stay away from The Coast and stick to the other side of Center Street while I made my escape back to my car.

"Um, Cyrus?" He didn't answer, but it sounded like all of the bikers on Folly were out in full force. Probably something to do with the Elbie incident.

I kept to the right side of the street and could see Cyrus dodging flying objects as he stood outside of The Coast. Siobhan and her sister had been here earlier in the evening. Was Maeve the source of all the pandemonium reigning tonight?

Amongst the bikers I spotted a couple of police officers.

"Cyrus," I shouted.

"Kell," he shouted back.

"Listen, pass the phone to Officer Jacoby," I shouted.

"No way, I ain't being seen conversing with no police," Cyrus shouted.

Bending down a bit, I peered through the small palm trees in the concrete island landscaping that divided this part of the street in half. Safely secluded from the chaos across the way, I tried again.

"Cyrus, this is an emergency! Just hand him your phone, you don't have to talk to him," I shouted, watching Cyrus making a move towards the entrance to The Coast. "Get back here! You're not hiding from me!"

He jumped away from the door and looked around. "I ain't hiding from you, Kell, you're not here!"

I crouched down a little lower. Okay, so it would be much easier to simply walk across the street and talk to the police in person, but I had a headache and just wanted to go home to bed. Maybe tomorrow would be a better day. With no dead bodies.

"One more second, Cyrus, and you're gonna be sorry," I threatened.

Exactly what he thought I was going to do, I have no idea, but it worked.

Cyrus held his phone at arms length and made motions with it to Officer Dan Jacoby, who was attempting to dispel with the unruly mob.

"Hello, this is Kell Palevac," I said quickly. "I can see you're busy and all, but there's a leg sticking out from some seaweed over at the beach. Thought you might need to check it out. Bye!"

"Hold on! Kell? What? Say that again," Officer Jacoby shouted.

I repeated myself and walked up the street towards my car. The police were just going to have to handle this one without me. Confident I'd given Jacoby proper directions on how to locate Hans, Linski and the leg, I started the engine and took off in the direction of home.

CHAPTER TWENTY

The director of my dreams was having his way with me again. I knew this because I've caught on to his little attempts to wreak havoc on my brain while I'm asleep. He didn't know who he was messing with. Okay, I may be blonde but I'm no dummy and his forays in to my dreamworld were beginning to piss me off.

"Kell, help find my killer," beckoned Dax Delaray with blood gushing from his forehead.

"Go away, you're dead," I shouted.

Dax sighed and wiped the oozing mess out of his eyes. "No shit, Sherlock. Now figure out who did this to me or there's gonna be more."

"I'm here, too, Dax," a breathy voice interjected.

"Who? Where," I strained to see the shadowy figure but could only make out one rather gross-looking leg.

"See, Kell, you better hurry up, I've already got company," Dax implored.

"So you two know each other? Who are you," I asked the leg.

A giant crab was clinging on to the leg with one claw and tearing the flesh off the foot of the leg with another.

"And just look what's happening to my pedicure," the leg screeched.

I screamed and Dax laughed and the leg screeched louder. I stopped screaming when I realized I was tangled up in my sheets at the foot of my bed. Fred and Sampson were side by side on the floor looking at me with terrified expressions.

Disentangling myself from the sheets didn't work too well and I rolled out of bed and landed next to my animals. Fred began slobbering on my face while Sampson delicately licked my hand. I scratched him and stood up.

"No worries, furry faces, it was just another stupid dream," I comforted my pets, glancing at the clock. The sun was beginning to appear and as it was apparently morning it was time to get up. I stretched and dismissed the dream director with a shake of my fist. Now that I'd done away with him I scooted to the bathroom.

The bathtub was filling with hot water laced with Epsom salt as I glanced at myself in the mirror. Last night had been surreal, and my eyes reflected the lack of sleep I'd had. Since I'd simply tumbled in to bed without washing my face they were also ringed with black smudges from the makeup I hadn't removed. I stuck my tongue out at my reflection and sank in to the soothing water, resting my head back on the neck pillow.

The fog in my head was shifting a bit and I remembered I had called Alex right before nodding off to inform her of the leg. I'd reached her voice mail and left all this information in a message, which she had been trying to return while I had been trying to sleep so I turned my phone off. Honestly, I was sort of expecting her to show up in person, but if she had I didn't hear the doorbell. There would be hell to pay for dissing my boss, but hey, didn't she know the stress I was under?

Lathering up my unruly hair and then dunking under to rinse cleared my head a bit more, so I loaded on the Conditioner Guaranteed To Work On Your Frizz and let it soak a few minutes. I peered at the bottle while I waited. Huh, there wasn't anything indicating a money back guarantee if the stuff didn't work. I dunked again and came up for air.

Normally I consider myself pretty fearless. My parents had raised me and my brother in a rather eclectic, bohemian lifestyle, traipsing from one end of the globe to the other and I'd seen a lot. Dead bodies did not factor into my area of expertise, although for the life of me I couldn't figure out why I seemed to keep finding them.

It didn't take a reporter to figure out the leg was part of an unfortunate dead body.

I was beginning to wonder whose.

The clicking noises from Fred's nails announced his arrival and I grabbed a fluffy white towel and dried off, pulling the plug on the bath water before he could try to get in the tub. He never actually makes it, but his front paws sometimes do and I was finished anyways.

"Hey there, fur face, let's go make some coffee and some phone calls," I suggested to Fred as I slipped my worn out purple robe on. We made for the kitchen.

While the coffee pot did its thing I turned my phone back on and found out I had nine missed calls. I scrolled through, recognizing Alex's number and Mid's and one or two or three from the chief. Uh oh. I don't think he's ever called me directly before. I decided to do the mature thing and call him back.

"Folly Beach police station," chirped a rather peppy voice for this early hour.

"Um, Connie? This is Kell Palevac, is the chief available," I asked.

"Kell! Thank the Lord you've called, Chief's been meaner than a hornet all mornin'," Connie whispered. "Been lookin' for you."

I took a deep breathe. "Well, can you please tell him I'd like to talk a minute," I said. My voice sounded nervous to my own ears and I squared my shoulders and began pacing my kitchen.

"Absolutely, honey, now don't go anywhere," Connie replied a bit more enthusiastically.

Deep breathe, pace, breathe, pace. I kept this up for what seemed an eternity until the chief finally made it to the phone.

"Ms. Palevac. How wonderful of you to come out of hiding," Chief Stoney said.

"What's that, hiding? No, sir, just home," I replied.

"Your phone must not be working," he said calmly.

I laughed. "Oh, no, I turned it off."

Silence. Chief Stoney was breathing kind of loud so I knew he was still there. I waited a bit.

"Um, Chief? Hello? I said I turned my phone off, I was so tired from all the commotion yesterday," I continued. "But it's back on now if you need to reach me."

I was intently inspecting a rather nasty looking bruise on my knee and wondering where it came from when he shrieked so loud I nearly dropped my phone.

"Are you out of your mind! You were tired? I've been up all night trying to get coherent answers out of a catatonic paranoid blubbering idiot and another imbecile who can't speak the English language," Chief Stoney hollered. I held my phone away from my ear and Fred growled at it.

"Yes, well, that would be Kenneth and Hans, I felt sure they were perfectly capable of relaying what happened," I said, crossing my fingers. "They're usually quite responsible."

"Capable? Responsible? Hah! Said you once again found a dead body and left them with it. The little guy is under observation as we speak," the chief yelled.

"Both your editor and I thought you were more professional than this!"

I scratched Fred and then I scratched my scar because it was starting to itch. "Is Kenneth alright?"

"Nothing a sedative won't handle. Cut to the chase, Ms. Palevac. Tell me everything," Chief Stoney barked.

He really seemed rather insistent and since I was grateful nobody bothered me in the middle of the night it seemed like a good idea to do what he asked. I focused and kept to the facts, culminating with the leg.

"So who is she," I asked.

"She? How do you know it's a female," the chief asked suspiciously.

"How many men walk around with pink polish on their toes," I retorted.

"Okay, it's a female. Pretty badly decomposed, nothing left of the face so they're running dental records," he responded.

Ugh, the image of a bunch of teeth in a faceless face made my stomach squirm.

I shook my head to dispel with the image before the dream director could take note.

The chief and I chatted a bit more, although he still sounded awfully mad.

"By the way, your editor said if I talk to you to tell you your ass is in big trouble and to call her immediately," Chief Stoney said a bit more cheerfully. "So good luck with that."

He disconnected and so did I. Shit. Time to deal with Alex DeWinter.

CHAPTER TWENTY ONE

My red Toyota Four Runner plodded slowly past the washout, sensing the person behind the wheel didn't really want to be heading in the direction of Center Street. Maybe automobiles had an innate sensory perception of their drivers. Mine seemed to have an easy time deciphering its owner, most likely because my lead foot was barely pushing the gas peddle. I idled a moment, letting my head rest against the steering wheel. The ocean splashed mellifluous sounds as the waves crept ashore and the sun was a peaceful burst of light high in the sky. I took a deep breath.

"How can I be in a bad mood with such a beautiful day going on," I asked the steering wheel. I raised my head. "I'm sure Alex will be understanding, I have nothing to be afraid of. In fact, this is going to be a great day."

The blast of a horn directly behind me snapped me out of my optimistic state pretty quickly. I wrenched my neck turning around to see who had the nerve to be in such a hurry in my little beach town.

"Hey, move your car," shouted the man behind the wheel of the vehicle behind me. He accented this request with another loud honk.

Tourists. Had to be, I didn't recognize anyone in the car and nobody around here is in a hurry to go anywhere. Before I could muster up a response the surfers standing around watching for waves descended upon the unsuspecting horn honker like a pack of vigilantes. They surrounded the car quickly.

"What's up, bro? What's the hurry," Harley asked the driver.

"Yeah, man, if you gotta honk your horn go back to Ohio, we don't like noise," said Mikee on the other side of the vehicle.

The tourists were looking a bit frightened now, so I leaned my head out of my window and granted leniency.

"It's okay, guys, I guess I should get out of the way," I hollered back at them.

"No worries. Bye!"

I put my car in gear and puttered away, checking my rear view mirror.

Surfers are generally a peaceful bunch, so I was pretty sure the Ohioans would escape unscathed. Folks learned when they came to Folly to slow down and enjoy island time. Either that or face off with angry locals. I sighed and continued on my way to work.

My mantra for the day was serenity. I kept reminding myself of this as I parked my car and snuck inside The Archipelago, where

Myra Glass greeted me with an expression that was anything but serene. Huh, I don't think I'd ever seen her frazzled before.

"Kell! Thank the Lord you're here! Alex has been meaner than a hornet," Myra whispered. "She's been waiting for you."

Something was familiar with this picture. I wrinkled my nose. Connie had just said the same thing about the chief. I squared my shoulders.

"Well, here I am," I said, smiling brightly. I patted Myra on the shoulder.

No worries!"

Myra's brows knitted themselves in to a frown above her wise little eyes, which she swiveled upward while muttering what seemed to be a silent prayer. I smiled at her again and boldly made for my desk.

"Serenity," I reminded myself, tossing my black bag on top of the mess.

"Serenity."

Sitting down, I gathered my unruly mop of hair in to a twist and secured it with my Celtic barrette, humming my mantra out loud while clearing a spot to rest my elbows. Chin in hands, I noticed Holly at her desk across from me with a smart- ass little grin on her face. Closing my eyes got rid of her and I continued my serenity pledge. Somewhere on the edges I could make out Holly's voice, light and trivial like a thistle bloom falling into silence without a sound, without any weight. When her tone of voice sounded like she was reprimanding a dog I opened my eyes and stared at her.

"What the hell are you babbling about," I asked.

"Why, Kell, I was saying how amazing it is that you showed up today," she said, shaking out her auburn curls. "After leaving poor Kenneth and Hans stranded with your latest dead person."

Our entertainment reporter Kevin Prentiss stopped typing at his desk next to hers.

"Really, Kell, you have certainly sullied your reputation around here, slumming with dead bodies," Holly continued. "I don't find it surprising one bit, considering your upbringing. You'd never find a true southern woman like me getting my hands dirty with such awfulness, it's really a disgrace." She stood up and walked to the coffee machine while I stared at her some more. Kevin shook his head and resumed typing.

Holly was still rambling words she might later regret while I contemplated my response. Her annoying voice kept going until I'd had enough.

"Park your tongue for a second, will you," I yelled at her. "Southern lady my ass, you were born ignorant and you've been losing ground ever since!"

"Why, I never! Need I remind you that you're the one who was born in some third-world country," Holly screeched, setting her cup of coffee on her desk and perching herself on the edge. "You and that heathen Siobhan, no wonder you get along so well!"

I pushed my chair back and stood up slowly, walking around to the front of my desk so we were only a few feet apart. Little lightning bolts of worry darted into her eyes even as she continued her rather brave attack.

"Now she's brought her sister here! Did you see the girl last night at Middleton's house?" Holly's voice was sharp and acidic and she held her head high as though sniffing something. "Such a tramp! The three of you make quite a trio, Kell."

She went on, blithely ignoring the sudden silence in the room, although I couldn't make out what she was saying because of the roar in my head. My right hand was balling itself into a fist when I was shoved rather unceremoniously to the side.

"No, Kell, this one's mine," roared the voice of an ancient Celtic warrior ready for battle. I tripped over two camera bags flung at my feet and fell in to Siobhan just as she tackled Holly and the three of us rolled around on the ancient linoleum floor. Fists were flying and words were flowing as we rolled ourselves right to the sharp points of some very high heels.

"Ouch," I yelled, rubbing my shin where one of the sharp-pointed shoes had struck.

"Bollocks," yelled Siobhan when another point collided with skin.

"Don't touch me," screamed Holly as she backed away, sliding on the linoleum as fast as she could.

Our editor was smiling at us in a controlled, rather unmirthful way which didn't quite reach her eyes, eyes that currently fixed the three of us in a blue-eyed vise. We waited. The silence stretched like a tightwire through the air. One spiked heel tapped its sharp-pointed toe. I glanced at Siobhan. She was shooting daggers with her eyes at Holly, who was curled up against the wall with her auburn curls sort of frizzy. I smiled.

With a quick intake of breath like someone about to plunge into icy water, Alex DeWinter directed her question at me through clenched teeth.

"Why so amused, Ms. Palevac?"

"Me? Nope, not me, Alex, um, Ms. DeWinter," I responded, keeping my voice soft and eminently reasonable. "You see, we were....."

"Shut up! Now! Before I fire your asses right here on the spot," screamed our editor in a voice that could cause a hearing impairment.

Holly whimpered and wiped crocodile tears from her baby blue, saucer like eyes. "I was attacked," she sniffed. I noticed a small, reddish mark blossoming on her cheek. Guess Siobhan made contact. I grinned and quickly sobered up before Alex spotted me again.

"Remember how Edgar was so very passionate about writing," I addressed Alex in my new soft voice. "We were all just, um, passionately discussing our respective articles and things got a bit, um, passionate."

Alex's glacial eyes melted as she focused on me once again. A rosy hint flushed her paper white complexion. "Why, yes, Kell, Edgar was so very passionate about his writing. Come, get off the floor and tell me all about this." She took my hand and sort of yanked me to my feet with a force not quite natural.

Siobhan looked at me from her spot on the floor and we rolled our eyes at each other.

"Come, Kell, to my office where we can discuss this," Alex said, guiding me away with an arm across my back.

"Wait! What about me? I was attacked! My hair is a mess and two of my fingernails are broken," Holly wailed, holding up a hand missing a couple of red tips. "I won't stand for this! I'll contact my attorney!"

Alex paused. "Holly, dear, why don't you take the day off, go get your nails fixed. My treat," she said with a wave of her hand. We continued towards her office.

"Well, okay," Holly replied brightly, her smile lighting her up from the inside like candles in a pumpkin. I wanted to squash her, but I plastered a pleasant grin on my face and rolled my eyes at Siobhan again, who was now upright and brushing her lanky body off.

Holly glanced warily in Siobhan's direction, scooted towards her desk and grabbed her Gucci bag, then quickly made her way to the door. Siobhan made a movement to follow so I gave her my best advice. "So not worth it."

She paused, nodding. As I walked away with my new best friend slash editor the unmistakable mutterings of ancient Gaelic rose in the air.

Siobhan was chanting what I recognized, thanks to my mom who taught me the language, an old Celtic curse, presumably directed at the dear, departed Holly. Her green, cat-like eyes were narrowed. I shuddered, happy to be able to call her friend and wondering what was in store for Holly.

Alex squeezed my shoulders as we reached her office. "Now, let's have ourselves a nice little chat about dear, dear Edgar."

This was probably better than being fired, I reminded myself as we entered the glass enclosure Alex called her office. "Sure, Alex, let's talk."

CHAPTER TWENTY TWO

"I've been buried alive, Kell, help me get out," pleaded the irritating voice of Dax Delaray. The little tinkling of a bell sounded from inside the sturdy looking wooden box a few steps in front of me. I moved towards it and saw a tiny brass bell connected to a string which fed through a small hole in the box. It jingled again.

"Please, Kell, help us," moaned another voice, a breathy young woman's, with an edge of desperation. "Let us out."

My body moved on its own accord closer and closer to the voices even though something was telling me to back up. I saw my hand reach down and slide the lid of the box over and then my hand was grabbed by another's and yanked inside. The lid slammed down.

"Oh, great, good job there, why did you pull her in here with us," the female voice asked in a very pissed-off fashion.

"Me? It wasn't me, I want out of here as much as you do," retorted Dax Delaray.

I squirmed around in the darkness, letting my eyes adjust so I could at least see something.

"Ring the bell again, you idiot," commanded the woman.

"Idiot? I certainly don't remember you talking to me like that before, in fact you begged for my attention," snorted Dax.

A patch of light showed through the darkness, illuminating the space somewhat. I turned over and found myself face to face with Jennifer Donnelly. I recognized her from her long blonde hair and the ugly red welt around her neck.

"It was me! I pulled you in here so you could be with all of us," Jennifer exclaimed. She scratched her forehead and the skin fell off. "You don't happen to have any lotion, do you?"

My body was frozen. I tried to run but there was no place to go and my legs didn't work anyways.

"Still haven't been able to help me out with these shitty holes in my hands, have you," asked Darla Simmons, raising her palms to me. She shook out her long blonde hair in disgust.

"Listen, can we just get out of here," asked Dax Delaray, stuffing his fingers in the hole in his forehead. "I've got a headache."

"At least you have a head! Mine is being reconstructed as we speak," shrieked the anonymous female.

I threw my head back and screamed a guttural cry of terror.

"Ouch!" Great, now I was going to have one hell of a bump where I'd collided with the wall behind my bed. At least my eyes were open, which meant I was awake and had escaped the dream director once again. The son-of-a-bitch was completely out of control now. My dead surfer girls were now joining Dax Delaray and my other unknown dead person in an attempt to scare the shit out of me. It was working. I huddled under the covers with Fred snoozing beside me. He obviously didn't feel like talking this early in the morning, so I picked up my cell phone from my bedside table and called Siobhan.

"Top of the mornin' to ya, Kell darlin'," she answered with her sing-song lilt.

"Care for a cuppa tea?"

"Maybe later, listen, I had this dream," I said.

Through the airwaves I could feel Siobhan brighten. "Ah, your dead people talking to you again, eh?"

"Why do they have to be my dead people? Do I have a magnet on me that says come to me all you dead people on Folly? Because I'm getting really sick of this shit," I complained. "Achoo!"

"God bless, you getting a cold," Siobhan asked.

I sneezed again. "I dunno, just woke up. Actually, my throat does feel kind of scratchy."

"Well, that's what you get for traipsing around town barefoot."

"That won't give you a cold."

"Sure it will, me Ma always said so."

"Well, my mom said it doesn't."

"Me ma raised nine of us."

"Bully for her," I retorted, raking my hair out of my eyes. "Who cares, do you want to hear my dream or not?"

"Go on, I'm listening," she instructed.

I started with the part about the little bell ringing.

"Ah," Siobhan interrupted. "That's from your conversation with Alex about Edgar Ellan Poe, where the dead were buried with a string attached to a bell, just in case they weren't really dead yet. Do you know family members sometimes would visit their loved ones for months after they passed, hoping to hear the bell ring?"

A heavy sigh escaped my lips just as another sneeze came on. "Yeah, don't remind me. I've heard enough about that man to last me ten lifetimes. Anyways, don't change the subject."

A shudder ran through me and Fred twitched in his sleep while I relayed my dream details. Siobhan kept encouraging me and I could feel her excitement raise a few percentage points when I reached the part about the head reconstructment.

"Hold up. Stop right there. Have you talked with Mid recently?" Her voice took on an ominous tone.

"No, I mean, he left me a message, but no. Why?"

"Write down this number."

"I've already got Mid's number."

"Don't be daft, I know you have Mid's number. Write this one down."

I complied, copying the local exchange with the accompanying digits on to a small pad . "So whose is it?"

"Her name is Special Agent Ruth Patella. She's a forensic artist with the South Carolina Law Enforcement Division. Call her," Siobhan instructed rather urgently.

"For what? I thought we were talking about my dream here," I replied.

Really, it was too early for all this. I needed coffee.

Siobhan's accent was getting thicker, which reminded me of Holly and what the chant was all about. "We are," she trilled sharply.

"I took her photograph yesterday for the article Mid's doing. She's reconstructing the face of the dead girl you found."

I swung my legs out of bed and made my way to the kitchen. "Seriously? So the woman in my dream is the dead girl? How's that happening?"

"Kell, you underestimate the powers of the subconscious mind and the powers of the dreamworld. Don't ask questions, call the lady," Siobhan commanded curtly.

"By the way, did you hear about poor Holly?"

"Not yet," I answered. "Hope she left the country."

"No such luck. Seems when she went to get her nails fixed yesterday the salon somehow glued her nails to the table with that stuff they use to apply tips. Poor dear lost a bit of skin when they pried her off," Siobhan said dramatically. "Had to be sedated."

So that's what the chanting was all about. I grinned. "Hope she's okay."

"She's fine, won't be able to type for a bit, so she won't be around the paper for awhile. Ah, well, these things have a way of working themselves out, ya know," Siobhan stated. I could feel her grin through the phone.

We hung up and I made coffee. My head was thick and I sneezed a bit more.

Definitely a cold coming on. Usually this will make me highly agitated because I can't do everything but right about now it was a welcome reprieve from rushing.

"Achoo," I sneezed and poured a cup, adding the cream and sugar. Sitting down with my pad and pen ready, I took a sip and dialed the number in front of me.

"Special Agent Patella here," answered a voice with a sweet edge to it.

Lucky day, these people generally don't answer the phone, at least the police I've dealt with. Guess Special Agent is way different. This one sounded nice, actually. I cleared my throat.

"Good morning, this is Kell Palevac with The Archipelago. Our photographer Siobhan gave me your number," I began.

An easy laugh invited me to share the happiness. "Oh, the sassy redhead? She and that handsome young man were by yesterday, but how can I help you?"

"I hear you're reconstructing the face of the woman from the beach. How do you do that and how far along are you," I asked, hoping she liked to talk.

I didn't need to worry. "Most of the time it's just the skull, but this one is still attached to the body so it's a bit cold, which makes it a little harder to push the pins in, but I should be finished by tomorrow," Special Agent Patella explained. "I'm not complaining, it's just that they keep those morgue rooms so icy. Brrrr."

I wrinkled my nose. "Pins?"

"Yes, I use tiny numbered push-pins that I insert into the skull to show tissue depth markers. They mark the spot to show how deep the modeling clay should be to approximate the victim's flesh," she continued. "My knowledge of muscle anatomy allows me to fill in the areas around the eyes, cheeks and lips. Yes, she's coming right along. Would you like to see her?"

Ugh. "Achoo," I sneezed. "Thanks very much, but I seem to be coming down with a cold."

The laugh was giddy now. "You don't need to worry, I don't think she'll catch it."

Ha ha ha. A funny dead person recreater. What the hell, I guess a sense of humor was a plus in her line of work. Special Agent Patella was excited to see the article in tomorrow's paper and I was excited to hear we'd have a face.

"But I thought they were running her dental records," I said.

"My understanding is they did, but no matches were found to link her to any of the missing persons file for unsolved cases. This should help," she replied.

We said our good-byes, but not before I was invited to come see her work anytime it was convenient for me. Hanging up, I made the quick decision that I wouldn't be visiting the morgue anytime soon.

CHAPTER TWENTY THREE

Fred, Sampson and I were lounging on my back porch, listening to the hullabaloo from the variety of birds outside. Trying to figure out which whoop, squawk, whistle and tweet belonged to who kept my mind off the rueful acceptance of the terrible knowledge that this might be the only solid reality in my shifting world. The whole strange dreamlike lunacy of things reminded me of the visitors from my sleep. Why in the world were these dead people messing with me? I attacked the dream with come good old fashion common sense, which lasted about ten seconds.

"I'm doomed to them bugging me, guys," I sighed. "Somebody better figure this mess out soon." I punctuated this with a loud achoo and sniffed indelicately.

"Achoo!" Upstairs someone echoed back. I looked up at the brown eye peering down through the planks of wood.

"Morning, Elbie," I greeted my neighbor. "Achoo!"

"Why're you copying me, Kell?"

"I'm not, I have a cold."

"Me, too! Now we can hang out together! My mom let me stay home from school," Elbie replied. "Uh, oh."

"Uh oh what," I asked.

The eye had disappeared, which was odd. I heard the squeak of the screened door and Elbie's voice came from off in the distance.

"I forgot I'm not allowed to hang out with you anymore, after you brought me to The Coast. My mom says that's not a place for kids," he hollered as the door snapped shut.

"Me? I didn't bring you there, you, oh forget it," I said. Why did Ludmilla always think I was the one getting her overgrown teenage son in trouble? I mean, Elbie doesn't exactly have both oars in the water. Huh, well if I was off limits then at least that was one way of escaping Elbie for the day. I planned on staying home, too.

Even though I kept telling myself not to think about the murder of Dax Delaray and the leg a cynical inner voice kept hounding me with questions. After spending some time returning work related phone calls that I couldn't really concentrate on, I pulled out a new puzzle and sat down at the kitchen table. I love puzzles. This one featured a little girl skipping on the beach. She was wearing a white ruffled tulle slip and soft wisps of hair fell across her face. The ocean was behind her and a shell or two were in the foreground. The image reminded me of the little baby I'd discovered and I wondered how she was. Maybe she'd grow up to skip along the shores of Folly, too.

While sorting the edge pieces for the outline of the puzzle I mulled over everything I knew about this mystery, letting my thoughts glide in and out. Dax Delaray had been an integral part of our little beach community and liked by most.

Last time I'd seen him alive was at the annual outdoor party Mazo's Market held in the streets out front of their building on East Ashley. I snapped a piece in place, completing one side of the puzzle. Everyone was dancing and now that I thought about it Dax had gotten into a fist fight of sorts with Lou Rinaldi. What had that been about?

"Why would Dax argue with the one guy on this island who's not only really big but from New Jersey," I mused outloud, fingering through the pieces. Another one fit and I was done with the top part. Oh, yeah.

"Because he was flirting with Lou's girlfriend Delores," I answered myself triumphantly. This reminded me what a lothario Dax had been, so I guess not everyone liked him. Snap. The puzzle pieces were coming together quite nicely.

The infant in the basket was indeed Dax's. Which brought me back to the question of who the mother was. Something was there, some answer, but I just couldn't find it. Suddenly the puzzle became annoying and thinking about Mazo's had reminded me of food so I got up and checked the fridge. Yep, same old same old. Nothing. I shut the door and called Mazo's for delivery service. It would be cheaper to drive there myself but I didn't feel like getting dressed. One good thing about catching a cold was an excuse to stay home.

I puttered around in my pajamas, dusting some shelves and rubbing lemon oil on my beautiful old oak-planked coffee table.

Blackbeard's large metal bird cage was still covered with the towel, so I did the right thing and pulled it off so he could face the day. He ruffled his colorful feathers and said good morning to me.

"I'm horny."

"Happy for you," I answered.

"Wanna have sex?"

"Nope," I said, my ears perking up as a rather loud achoo echoed down from the vent above. Elbie really was sick.

"Show me your hooters," Blackbeard demanded.

"Nah, sorry, maybe Siobhan will sometime," I told him. "Can't we please learn some nice words?"

"Off with their heads!"

I turned my back on the mouthy feathered creature and walked to the door to answer the ringing of the bell. Food. The delivery guy looked familiar.

"Here ya go," he said, handing me the brown bag and the bill. I stared at him.

Shaved bald head, long braided goatee, completely sleeved arms. Tattoo man from the surf shop.

"Hey, I thought you worked at the surf shop," I said, taking the bag from him. "We had lessons one time."

He stared at me with blue eyes hidden under thick, yellow brows. "Oh, yeah dude, I remember, Trista told me about that, uh, lesson," he said with a grin that brought out the creases in his tanned face. "I do this for extra cash."

I held out my hand. "Kell Palevac."

"Myron Pringle." We shook.

"Funny, you don't look like a Myron," I said.

"Parents' fault," he replied.

"Gotcha," I nodded, handing him some cash. "Keep the change."

Myron turned to leave and then stopped. "Who's the dude hiding in the bushes across the street?"

"Huh?" I peaked around him out the front door. "Where? I don't see anybody?"

He raised his hand to shield the sun. "Dude, I totally saw a dude in the bushes. Gone now."

We both looked left and right but there was nobody around. Maybe someone was using the bushes as a rest stop. It happens.

"Probably nothing. Well, thanks again, bye," I said. He lifted a hand in farewell.

I shifted the brown bag to my hip and locked the door behind him. Probably nobody hiding in the bushes, but better safe than sorry. The idea of feeling vulnerable on my cozy little island was infuriating and I plopped the bag down a little too hard on my white-tiled countertop. The loud thwack that ensued along with the sticky orange stuff puddling quickly confirmed I'd broken something.

Hmmm. The small bottle of orange juice was history.

"Oh, well, who needs orange juice," I grumbled. Achoo. Oh, yeah, me. I cleaned the mess up and put away the other essentials I'd purchased to get me through the day. I stuck the wine in the fridge. And night. I wasn't planning on driving anywhere.

The afternoon passed by and I was feeling confined but still not ready to venture off. Munching on an apple dispeled with some of the nervous energy currently flowing through my body but not all of it. Maybe the last few rays of sunshine would help. I grabbed a beer, Fred's leash and my keys. Fred was standing by the window looking outside, which was rare. Usually he's asleep. We stood there for a bit, both of us staring out the window. I scratched his ear.

"Look, buddy, for some reason I don't think we should venture off to the beach," I told him. "Let's go out back on the dock."

I paused at the fridge and took a piece of frozen chicken neck out in case we felt like crabbing. We passed through my back porch and out through the gate to the backyard, which ended at the small wooden structure practically in the marsh. The wooden boards are old and frayed and the ramp creaked as we made our way down to the floating dock beneath. The tide was coming in, carrying with it the blue crabs I decided to try and catch. Fred eased his monstrous body under the ramp to escape the last of the sun's rays and I sat down with my legs dangling off the edge. I leave a piece of string with a metal weight attached to it tied to a cleat. I pulled it up and secured the chicken neck, tying it off with a quick yank, then gently lowered the string down in to the salty water.

The dark, soft pluff mud cushioned the hard craggy oyster beds poking out along the marsh grass. I closed my eyes and took a deep breathe, inhaling the swampy, earthy smells of the low country. They say the distinct odor of pluff mud is a result of the bacteria, water content and climate conditions. I opened my eyes and reached down, scooping a bit with my fingers. The silky texture was deceiving. The stuff will pull you in and suck your shoes right off your feet. Trust me, I lost a perfectly good pair of sneakers learning this.

Fred was snoring, competing with the cicadas to see who was the loudest. The downy white feathers of the egret resting on the marsh bank were so close I could maybe reach out a hand and stroke them. With a swiftness that belied his awkward neck he plunged his beak down in the water, emerging with a small striped bass. I watched transfixed as the bird swallowed the fish, gulping hard to fit the thing down his throat. The outline of the doomed sea creature stood out against his thin neck and then it was gone, I was guessing straight to his stomach.

"That was wild," I said. "Fred, you really should wake up and watch all of this, it's beautiful." He groaned and shifted in his spot under the ramp and continued to snore. "Your loss, fur face."

The long-handled net was in reach. I grabbed it with my left hand and slowly raised the string up with my right. There was a gentle tug, which meant someone was eating my bait. Easing the string up a bit more, I spotted a small blue crab munching away. A quick pull and the swoop of the net and he was mine.

"You're too little," I told him, inspecting the beautiful blue claws tinged with orange. "Go back and grow up." I let him out of the net and watched as he scooted sideways, claws drawn, until he fell over the side of the floating dock and back to his watery home.

The tide was coming in quickly and the first shadows of the night were beginning to gather. I gulped my beer in long swigs, listening to the musical medley of nature. Behind me something made a whimpering sound.

"Shit!" I scurried backwards. The tide certainly had come in fast, so fast in fact that the floating dock had risen a good bit, pinning Fred underneath the ramp.

"Come on out, buddy. Wiggle!"

He wiggled and I pulled and he emerged unscathed, except for a few hairs stuck in the wood. I hugged him and he sat down in my lap, which meant I was in dire jeopardy of being squished. When I was certain he'd recovered from his near death fiasco we stood up and made the treck back to the house.

CHAPTER
TWENTY FOUR

Sleep eluded me. Maybe my brain was too wired to fall victim to the dream director once again, or maybe Fred's snoring kept me awake. The nasty cold I'd caught could also be to blame, I decided, with a sneeze. I splashed my face with water and toweled dry, peering at my reflection in the bathroom mirror. Little purple smudges shaped like half moons had made homes underneath my eyes which were so bloodshot I looked hungover. Even after two cups of coffee my head felt cloudy and my body was so achey all I wanted to do was crawl back in bed.

It was quite easy convincing myself this was an excellent idea, so I huddled back under my covers and dialed The Archipelago. Myra Glass answered on the second ring.

"Hey there, Myra, this is Kell, I'm calling in sick today. Can you please tell Alex," I asked.

"Poor dear, do you have a fever? Would you like me to bring you anything," Myra responded soothingly.

I sniffled. "I dunno, my nose is really stuffed though. And no, I ordered from Mazo's yesterday so I should be fine, thanks."

"Well, dear, take care of yourself, we'll manage here without you for the day," Myra said.

I sniffed again, sneezed and disconnected, silencing the ringer on my phone. Talking to Myra made me miss my mom. She was all the way over in Russia doing research for a book about Rasputin, who had apparently been quite prolific and had left behind many children, now grown and eager to talk about days gone by. I sighed, turning over and pulling the covers over my head a little to block out the light.

Rain humming down on the roof woke me up from a wonderfully dreamless nap that seemed to last for hours. I glanced at the clock, rubbing my eyes. Yep, hours alright. It was now late afternoon. The sun had been up when I went back to bed but now the clouds had rolled in along with the wind blowing against the windows. I stretched and rolled out of bed. It felt good making up for the lost night's sleep. My stomach was growling so I pulled a slice of cold pizza out of the fridge and poured a glass of milk, munching and sipping until I was full. Fred and Sampson were both looking at me so I decided to feed them, too. I was pouring Fred's food into his doggie bowl when the there was a knock on my front door.

I glanced out the window but no cars were outside, so I peeked through the peephole. Raindrops were coming down on the person standing there and I recognized him with a bit of surprise.

"Charles," I greeted him, opening the door. "Well, hello. What are you doing here, I didn't even know you knew where I lived."

Charles Heyward was standing outside holding a bag in one hand and shielding his eyes from the rain with the other. "Sorry for the unannounced visit, I was in the area and thought I'd stop by."

Considering the washout was a few blocks to my right and the old Coast Guard Station another couple to the left I was trying to figure out where in the area he'd been exactly. "Um, Kell? I'm getting awfully wet out here. Mind if I come inside?" Charles wiped the rain out of his eyes and handed me the bag.

"Oh, sorry, sure, come on in," I said, attempting to smooth back my unruly mop of hair and wishing I'd put a little makeup on. "What's in the bag?"

Charles shrugged out of a soggy tan canvas jacket and shook his wet hair out of his eyes. "Coronas. I know they're your favorite."

He did? "Gosh, thanks, come on in the kitchen and dry off a bit. What brought you to my neck of the woods," I asked.

I took the beer out of the bag along with a lime and a bottle of whiskey.

Hmmmm. Was there a party going on at my house I'd missed the invitation to?

Grabbing a knife, I sliced the lime in wedges and stuck a slice in two beers, handing him one. Our eyes met. His washed out shade of blue was lighter than usual, giving him an oddly spooky appearance.

"Cheers," he said, clinking his bottle with mine.

We took long swigs and sat in silence for a minute. "So, I'm happy to see you, Charles, just a bit taken aback. We haven't really talked in years." I shifted in my chair and scratched Fred, who had graced us with his presence, most likely looking to see if the guest had brought any food.

"I know, that's why I wanted to stop by and catch up a little bit, Kell. I've missed you," Charles said with such intensity my face felt warm. His full lips curved in to a smile that couldn't quite dispel with his sneer and didn't seem to reach his eyes, eyes staring at me with a degree of concentration so elevated I was sure he could read my mind. "How's the detective work going? Any leads?"

I broke free of his gaze and walked to the fridge. "What? Oh, you mean about Dax Delaray and the woman? Nah, I've had lots of phone calls from islanders but most are easy to figure out if you know who's feuding with who. They're just trying to rat on each other. How about some cheese and crackers," I asked, turning back around.

The rain was steady now, as sharp as a lance against the windows. A swirl of greasy fog swept by and was split in half by a spike of lightening. There was a flash, like light caught in water, when our eyes met. Charles was staring at me from way inside himself like an animal looking out from the brush.

"What," I asked as nervous little flutterings pricked my chest. "I know I must look a wreck. I've got this damn cold and I wasn't exactly dressed for company."

My flustered little laugh caught in my throat and I sneezed, setting the block of cheese and box of crackers down on the table. Another long drink of my corona soothed my throat.

"What woman," Charles asked, gulping his beer down and reaching for another. "One for you?"

"Well, sure," I agreed.

Since he seemed interested in my story I went ahead and gave him the details of the leg, which was indeed female, and how we'd have a face soon to identify her with. When I was finished I got up and walked to the window, opening it up to let in some fresh air. The rain slashed out and blew a ferocious breeze that felt like a knife in my lungs but I'd noticed Charles had little beads of perspiration on his upper lip so I figured he must be warm. He kept rubbing his tongue against the back of his teeth in a rather unsettling manner and a flicker of a smile rose at the edges of his mouth and then died out. Without any warning he snatched the bottle of whiskey and knocked back a long shot. He sat with his left forearm resting on his knee, his hand grasping the bottle tightly and his head hung forward. He took another drink and set the bottle down, pulling a pack of cigarettes out of his shirt pocket. He pulled one out, lit it and eyed me through the flame of the match.

"Um, I don't have an ashtray," I said a bit insulted. Usually guests ask if they can smoke in my house, which is a no, but Charles seemed tightly wound and I didn't want him unraveling in my kitchen. He stood up and made the short walk to the sink, tapping ashes on top of my dirty dishes.

"This is great, absolutely wonderful," he said, his voice cracking with a sardonic weariness.

"Charles? Are you alright," I asked, a strange wave of grayness washing over me. "What do you mean?"

"That fucking bitch! She screwed up my whole life! Hah, screwed everybody is more like it!" The words were sudden and raw and very angry. I stood up and raised my eyebrows.

"Charles! Who are you talking about? Come on, you're making me kinda nervous here," I said.

My front door burst open and two figures spilled in to the room. I twirled around just in time to see Siobhan and Maeve tumble inside and catch the excited words pouring out of Siobhan's mouth.

"Kell, you won't believe it! The face was finished during the night and she's been identified! Kell, listen, you'll never in a million years guess whose girlfriend she was." She was talking so fast I barely heard it all. She was barreling towards me with Maeve closely behind when she stopped suddenly. Her sister's black hair fell foreword so it meshed with her reddish locks and they stood together like a pair of mythical goddesses dropped to earth.

A strong masculine arm encircled my neck and I felt the familiar jab of cold steel in my back. I tried to turn my head around. The arteries in Charles's neck were pulsating and he gave a yank that made me decide to hold still.

"Ahhh, just what I've always wanted. A blonde, a brunette and a redhead," he sneered, his whiskey breath laced with cigarettes. "Everyone in the bedroom!"

CHAPTER TWENTY FIVE

Oh, hell, I thought crankily as melodramas filled my head. Through the disconnected thoughts two facts stood out as I experienced a dazzling leap of logic. I should never had allowed Charles inside and we were now in a whole lot of trouble.

How was I to know? Not one person on this entire island had even alluded that this man was a suspect. Maybe this was some sort of a joke Siobhan and her sister were playing on me.

"Bollocks, Charles, have you lost your mind? Put the gun down and let's see if we can sort this out, shall we," Siobhan suggested with her affable Irish inflection.

She took a step forward. The click of the trigger echoed in my ears and the metal rested against my head. Okay, so this wasn't a joke.

Charles' voice sounded tight and faraway. "You know, Siobhan, you never did follow rules very well. You two wenches have exactly one second to walk to the bedroom before I blow her head off."

Right about now I was really hoping Siobhan would just shut the hell up and listen for once in her life. I was also hoping her sister wasn't as stubborn as she was.

Maeve was scrutinizing the situation with her blazing violet eyes. She took hold of her sister's arm.

"Right then, is this the way? Let's go have a seat in Kell's bedroom," Maeve said with her sensual lilt. Her voice sounded programmed to thaw out the worst of situations. I was hoping this was one of them.

"Walk," Charles commanded, jabbing the gun in my back. So much for that idea. I followed the other two with Charles behind me. We entered my room and he slammed the door shut, clicking the lock in place. He motioned with the gun for us to sit on my bed so we sat.

"For the love of God, Kell, if you'd answer your damn phone none of this would be happening," Siobhan seethed.

"My phone's been turned off. If you haven't noticed I've got a nasty cold and I was resting," I spat back.

"Resting? Lucky you, I was up all last night with Special Agent Patella finishing the head," she pronounced.

"Bully for you, how is this all my fault? What does my phone have to do with anything," I growled.

"If you had any sense you'd leave your phone on, then I could've reached you and told you about this ingrate," she declared.

Charles pointed his gun at Siobhan and took a gulp out of the whiskey bottle.

"Sorry, Charles, this has all been such a shock," she said with a wave of her hand. "But, really, Kell, how irresponsible are you anyways?"

"Me? You've got nerve, Siobhan," I said, leaning forward. "Who's the one knocking back drinks at The Coast in the middle of a work day?"

"As I recall you were right there with me," she fumed, leaning forward.

"From what I can tell Irish people ignore anything they can't drink or punch," I yelled.

From her position in the middle of us Maeve held out her arms and nudged us back in our places. "Iosa, Mhuire's a Iosaif! Stop it, the both of you!"

Charles pointed the gun at Maeve. "What'd you say?"

"Jesus, Mary and Joseph," Siobhan and I said in unison.

He lowered the gun with a smirk. "Nah, they aren't helping you here. I suggest ya'll shut the hell up."

Siobhan and I both opened our mouths and Maeve elbowed us. Hard.

"Ouch, Maeve, that hurt," Siobhan moaned, smacking her sister's arm away.

"Shut up!" Charles, Maeve and I yelled in unison. This was my second time being held hostage and I was learning it was awfully important to agree with ones captor. Especially one with a gun in one hand and a bottle of whiskey in the other.

Our jailor breathed an exasperated sigh and sunk to the ground in front of us, his back against the wall. His face was so clear it was almost bloodless and had such a haunted look to it I barely recognized the young man who had played football when we were in college. When he spoke his voice had an edge of desperation to it.

"This is not how this was going to be. It was stupid of me to come here," Charles said. "I should be making my getaway. Why'd that sorry excuse for a girlfriend have to wash up on the beach. She should've stayed way out in the ocean where I dumped her."

Okay, he was talking. This was good. I honed my reporting skills and did what I do best.

"You know, Charles, the three of us are completely clueless about all of this.

You say you dumped her in the water? What's her name?" I kept my line of questioning casual and easy.

"Her name is Fran Churchill, that's what I was here to tell you. She's from London and was here last summer working at Dax's restaurant. Once her face was completed people recognized her," Siobhan interjected.

Charles' face started to fill back up with blood, he twisted his mouth in to an ugly sneer and his eyes narrowed ominously.

"Siobhan, if you don't mind, I was asking Charles," I said through clenched teeth. "Go ahead, Charles."

His features relaxed a bit and I breathed a little sigh of relief. "Yeah, she's right. Her name's Fran, we met last summer while she worked for that scum bucket Delaray. Hey, if I'm going to be telling this story let's all grab a beer," he said, standing up.

"Great idea, let's head to The Coast," Siobhan exclaimed with a clap of her hands.

Charles pointed the gun at her. "What do I look like, some kind of moron?

Kell, go get the Coronas and get back in here."

He unlocked the door and watched me walk to the fridge and take out the beer and lime. I reached for the little knife I'd been using earlier to slice with.

"Forget the knife," he said.

"But you can't drink it without lime slices," I argued.

"You can now. Get your ass back in here, Kell, I am not in a very good mood," he growled. My ass moved quickly and sat back down on my bed.

Charles handed us each a beer and opened one for himself. "So, as I was saying, we dated all summer long, exclusively so I thought, but that womanizer wouldn't leave her alone. Not enough that he was screwing around with most of the waitresses, he had to have Fran, too. Oh, she denied it, all the way up until she had the baby. One look at the kid and my suspicions were confirmed. Me, blonde and blue eyed. Dax, dark hair and dark eyes. Baby, the spitting image of her father."

We sat there in silence for a moment. Charles seemed lost in his thoughts. I needed him to tell the rest of the story.

"Um, go on Charles, it's good to get it all out. So what happened," I asked as soothingly as possible. The three of us swallowed our beers in sync while we waited on our captor to bring us up to speed.

His eyes were practically colorless and his weariness was growing, but the flood gates had opened and the torment was finding its way out. "I never meant to kill that jerk! Oh, trust me, it crossed my mind but I only brought the gun to scare him. Bastard had to get all cocky and shit and before I knew it, boom!"

Charles accentuated this by pointing his gun and imitating actually shooting it. The three of us ducked. My eyes met Siobhan's and she mouthed a silent what do we do now to me. I shook my head and shrugged.

"Why did you want to see Dax," I asked.

"I wanted to catch him off guard, so I drove to the beach early that morning and stopped him while he was biking. Idiot tried to get away from me on the beach.

I showed him his daughter and told him he had to help out financially. He laughed at me. Told me to take the kid back to the whore who spit her out," Charles said, the whiskey slurring his speech. "I pointed the gun at him and it went off."

"Pretty good shot there, Charles. If I remember it was straight to the forehead," Siobhan said, toasting him with her Corona.

He pointed the gun at her. "I told you I didn't mean to shoot him, I just wanted to scare him!"

"I believe you. We believe you," I said, elbowing Maeve who echoed my statement. "Right, Siobhan?"

"Oh, but of course. Sorry, Charles," she replied quickly.

Charles lowered the gun. "Where was I?"

"You just shot Dax Delaray," Siobhan reminded him.

His face twisted a bit and his sneer intensified. "Yeah, so then I got spooked by the old lady and the dog, so I left the baby and ran. Well, I sort of hit the lady and maybe shot the dog. Anybody know how they're doing?"

"They're recovering just fine," I said. "Go on."

"But what happened to Fran Churchill? How many people have you killed, Charles," Siobhan asked. I rolled my eyes and pinched the bridge of my nose. If she could just shut up and let me be the reporter.

The flash of lightening illuminated my room and lit Charles' eyes up like an arsonist. The gun was trained on the three of us now. The words that came out of his mouth were tight and controlled.

"Ladies, it's not important how many people I've killed. It's important how I get along with the people still alive."

I nodded my head vigorously. "Exactly, which is why I'm so happy you decided to come here and tell me your story. Please,

Charles, what happened to Fran," I asked, knowing my persistent reporter's questions might get us killed.

He stared at me for a moment, his eyes haunted and helpless looking below eyebrows knotted together in confusion. I'd never cared much for this arrogant blue-blooded Charlestonian but right now he appeared so vulnerable I felt a momentary twinge of sorrow. Well, until the shiny glint of the gun reminded me why we were here. He raked his dirty blonde hair through his fingers.

"We'd been staying in the guest house on my parents' property downtown," he began, his words so soft I had to lean forward a bit to listen. "They're over in Europe until Christmas. None of the staff thought it was strange for me to stay out back, I like to be alone away from the big house and nobody spotted Fran or the baby. I kept them inside."

I raised my eyebrows and he shrugged his shoulders. "Had to be that way. I stayed with Fran over in London until the baby was about due, then we flew here because she wanted the kid to be born in America. Yeah, I was gonna have a great surprise for my folks when they returned, a grandchild, but we see how that turned out," he said with a snort.

"When I told Fran I was going to confront Dax, show him the baby and tell him to pay child support she went crazy," he continued, blowing out an exasperated breathe. "We struggled and she fell, hit her head on the table. I left her there that morning and when I got back she was, well, gone."

"Gone," I asked.

"Dead," he replied. "So I wrapped her up in an old oriental rug and took her out to sea in my parents' boat. I dumped her pretty far out there but I guess she just had to make it back to Folly one last time."

"This place does have a mystical draw to it," Siobhan commented. Charles fixed her with a quizzical expression and shook his head.

"None of this was supposed to happen! I was going to do the right thing and marry her, but somehow I knew the kid wasn't mine and I was right," he said emphatically. "Enough of this story! I need another beer."

CHAPTER TWENTY SIX

"Off with their heads! Show me your knockers! I'm horny! Wanna have sex?"

Charles spun around and pointed the gun at my bedroom door. "Who the hell is that?"

I took the opportunity to try to get us at least out of the room. "It's my parrot, who is really hungry. Can I go feed him?"

"Show me your hooters," Blackbeard squawked loudly.

Charles unlocked the door and motioned with the gun for the three of us to get up. We scurried out before he could change his mind.

"Off with their heads!"

I walked over to Blackbeard's cage with Charles at my heels. He pointed the gun at my parrot. "Feed him and get him to shut up before I blow his head off."

Hmmm. I hesitated a moment. The bird was utterly annoying, foul-mouthed and noisy as hell. "I'm horny!"

I heard the click of the trigger and moved fast, dispensing some parrot kibble to the pain in the ass before he got feathers all over my house. Charles turned and walked back to the kitchen where Siobhan and Maeve were sitting at the table.

"Hurry up and get back over here with the rest of us," he commanded as I shook the food out.

Above my head I could hear my teenage neighbor through the vent. He was chanting some sort of gibberish only he could understand.

"Elbie," I said in a muted whisper. Blackbeard cocked his head to the left.

"Elbie," he squawked loudly.

"What," came the response from above.

I stared at Blackbeard and he stared back at me. He'd never said Elbie's name before. I looked over my shoulder. Charles was engrossed in a conversation with Maeve. Siobhan met my eyes and nodded at me so I kept going.

"Call police," I said quietly.

"Call police," Blackbeard whooped. Charles turned around in his chair.

"What the hell is going on over there," he asked, pointing the gun in my direction. Maeve reached out a hand and placed it on his arm.

"Nothing to worry about, the bird talks to himself all day long," she said soothingly. "He repeats what he hears on the television. Silly creature was watching an episode of Cops. Please, Charles, tell me more about your family." Her eyes were pools of wine I could easily drown in. Charles turned back to her and as I watched he appeared to be melting a bit around the edges. Was the intoxicating Maeve working her magic? He took another pull from the whiskey bottle. Hey, whatever worked.

"Ya want me to call the police," Elbie asked from upstairs. I cringed but nobody else seemed to hear him, so I scooted away and walked over to the table.

"Call police," Blackbeard cackled. "Call police, call police!" I stopped and scurried back to the cage, covering it with the blanket.

"Nighty night," I whispered.

Charles had the gun trained on me as I made my way over to him. "Good idea, Kell."

His eyes were drooping a bit and he'd made it about half way through the bottle of whiskey. Maeve began singing in a voice so mesmerizing I was sure we'd all fall asleep.

"Over in Killarney many years ago, me Mither sang a song to me in tones to sweet and low," she began, her velvety murmur echoing in the quiet of the night.

"Too-ra-loo-ra-loo-ral, too-ra-loo-ra-li. Too-ra-loo-ra-loo-ral, hush now don't you cry."

My body was exhausted from the nasty cold and all this excitement but I had to stay alert. I glanced at Siobhan. She motioned with her head towards Charles and I nodded. He was slowly dozing off, the gun in his hand resting lightly on the counter.

"Too-ra-loo-ra-loo-ra, too-ra-loo-ra-li. Too-ra-loo-ra-loo-ral, that's an Irish lullaby." The melodious sounds wove a languid web of tranquility around the room as I eased my hand towards the gun. In the midst of the quietness I heard the click of my front door being unlocked.

A figure tumbled in to the room, dressed in full police regalia and toting a pistol in each hand. It came to a sudden halt and pointed the guns in our general direction. "Nobody move! I swear I'll blow the heads off of every mother-fuckin' last one of ya!"

Charles snapped to just as I grabbed his gun. "Wait, help me! Maeve, help," he pled to his songstress.

"Pog mo thoin!" Siobhan and Maeve shouted in unison, tackling Charles to the ground as I held the gun far away.

Elbie lowered his pistols. "What'd they say?"

"Kiss my ass," I translated. "Achoo!"

EPILOGUE

The sun rose, a peaceful burst of light across the primrose sky. Marvelous swanlike clouds scudded playfully by but the sun stood proud and the misty white wisps evaporated like ghostly apparitions. The ocean flowed in and covered my feet.

I stood still for a few moments, letting the cool water come and go with the tide. It's something I'd done since I was a child, remaining in one spot and letting the sand wash out from under my feet until my heels were so low I almost fell backwards.

Just about when it felt like my calves were stretched to their limits I eased my feet out of their sandy niches and turned my back on the powerful Atlantic.

A group of surfers walked past me as I made my way back to my car. One had on a Santa Claus outfit and the others appeared to be disguised as elves.

"What's up? Can you really surf in these get-ups," I asked.

One of the elves smirked and said, "Dude, I can ride my stick wearing anything."

"Or nothin' at all," shouted another elf, bending over and mooning me.

"Hey, Merry Christmas," Santa shouted over his shoulder as the group made their way towards the waves.

"Same to ya'll," I said with a smile.

A few months had passed since the Charles episode and the island was in the holiday spirit. Tiny white lights adorned every palm tree and mistletoe hung in some very inventive spots. Scary Harry had, well, scared me the last time I walked in to Mazo's Market. I was hardly inside when he grabbed me and gave me a slobbery smooch. Instinctively my fist balled up to knock him upside his head when he pointed up at the mistletoe hanging in the doorway. Most of the locals knew about his scheme by now, but I shudder to think what an unsuspecting tourist would do if kissed.

The car was warm from the morning sun and I idled there at the washout for a moment. A couple of local ladies were out for a brisk walk and we waved at each other. They, too, appeared to be in holiday mode. One was dressed in green and the other in red and both sported burgeoning baby bumps under their festive attire.

Another woman had a rather large surfboard balancing on her head as she passed in front of my car, her round belly leading the way towards the water. Huh, I didn't know you could surf while pregnant.

"Maeve, you certainly lived up to your reputation," I whispered, pulling out on to East Ashley.

Brilliant flashes of sunlight bounced off the windshield and I almost passed by Santa Claus hitchhiking a little ways up the road. Even though he was dressed all in red and covered with a white flouncy beard I recognized my biker buddy. Cyrus was holding a Santa hat in one hand and sticking his thumb out with the other. His shiny bald head resembled an ornament and his heavy black motorcycle boots gave him a real Folly Beach Santa Claus edge. I pulled over and he lumbered in.

"Thanks, Kell, this suit is killin' me here," Cyrus mumbled through the fluffy cotton stuck to his face. I pulled on a piece of the beard.

"Ow, cut it out," he bellowed, swatting at my hand.

"Why'd you glue it on," I asked with a grin.

"How else was I supposed to make it stick," he answered indignantly.

"Anyways, I gotta get to the library. I'm the star of breakfast with Santa Claus."

I laughed and he glared at me so I composed myself. "Very nice of you to volunteer."

Cyrus let out something between a snort and a sigh. "Community service."

"Aah," I acknowledged. "I'm on my way to the Mayor's house to catch up with Bonnie and the baby, can you stop with me first?"

Cyrus sat up straight and pulled some white fluff away from his mouth. "Hell, no, not if the Mayor's there, he's been lookin' for me, don't know what for but he's lookin'."

I slowed down to say hello to the Stringers who were waving at us a bit frantically. "I'm sure he's gone to work already. Say hello to the Stringers."

Jacob Stringer's thin gray hair was combed over neatly and his glasses perched on the end of his crooked nose. He pushed them up and presented his wife to us as if we'd never met before. "Behold, it's a miracle! Thirty years of marriage and no children, now look!"

Delia Stringer blushed and place a hand on the obvious swell of her belly. Her long gray braid hung foreward and brushed the top of the bump. Her startling blue eyes met mine and the heavy creases around them blossomed as she gave us a broad smile. "We've been blessed."

"Congratulations you two," I shouted as we pulled away. I turned towards Cyrus. "Sort of like Abraham and Sarah from the bible."

He twisted his blockish neck from side to side. "How in the hell did that happen, aren't they like, old?"

"Cyrus, I don't know exactly what has happened here either, but this whole flippin' island seems pregnant," I said with a shrug.

"It's that sister of Siobhan's," he answered matter of factly. "Maybe she put something in the water, or maybe she cast a spell. Probably a spell. I mean, Siobhan won't stop chantin' that nonsense of hers all the time, sister's just the same."

I shifted gears. "Who knows, Cyrus, but this place is exploding with people expecting babies."

"Yep," he agreed. "Need some fresh blood around this town. Real locals."

We pulled up to the McLeod's house, the tires grinding the oyster shells so the driveway had a little dusting of white powder hovering in the air. The menagerie that greeted us was outfitted in a variety of holiday ensembles. I scratched the head of a furry poodle wearing antlers and Cyrus let a scruffy beagle sporting a Santa cap lick his outstretched hand.

"Hey, we match," he said to the dog, plopping his own hat in place on his shiny head.

We walked around back to the dock. From a distance I could make out Bonnie, Lurlene Higgenbottom, Miss Betty and Tusk. The squeal of a little one assured me the baby was there, too.

"Slow down, Kell, this damn suit is hot," Cyrus grumbled. "It's Christmas time, it's supposed to be cold."

"Yeah, well, it's Folly," I said as we reached the end of the dock.

Tusk raised his large head and regarded me with his solemn blue eyes as I took a seat on the bench next to his master. I gave Miss Betty a long squeeze and felt her narrow shoulders in my arms. Lurlene and Bonnie sat on the bench beside us.

In keeping with the miracles of the holiday season the child was perched on Bonnie's lap.

"What a glorious morning! Isn't it simply dazzling," Bonnie asked, jostling the baby up and down a bit too enthusiastically. Lurlene's brow furrowed and her mouth puckered so I reached out and motioned for the infant. Bonnie handed her over with impressive speed and jumped to her feet, brushing imaginary fuzz off her jeans.

"It's a beautiful day," I agreed, studying the miniscule creature on my lap.

Dark wisps of hair sprung like miniature ringlets on the tiny head and eyes as primitive as the first rays of dawn studied me with a calm expectancy. "She's darling, aren't you Gracie Mae?"

Gracie Mae McLeod Delaray rewarded me with a joyous beam and a bright giggle. She certainly bore a striking resemblance to her father, and I wondered how much she took after her mother, who had met an untimely death at the hands of Charles Heyward. He'd made a full confession to the police and was currently sitting in a jail cell awaiting trial.

The teak cane resting against Miss Betty's knee was just within reach of Gracie's outstretched chubby fist and she patted it like a favorite toy. "Sent straight from heaven," the old lady murmured.

"So, Lurlene, this baby livin' with you?" Cyrus posed the question and made goofy faces under his Santa hat at the child. Gracie giggled and cooed. If I had a camera Cyrus would never hear the end of this but I didn't so I saved the image in my memory to tell later at The Coast.

"Yes, well, she'll be between my house and her aunt's," Lurlene said. "She'll be very well taken care of."

Bonnie was rocking a miniature Chihuahua in her arms, looking back and forth between those of us gathered on her dock. "They say it takes an island to raise a child," she exclaimed cheerfully.

"So you were born here, and the island's gonna take care of you," Cyrus said to Gracie Mae with a nod. "Somethin' wild about that. I'm sure glad all the commotion died down around here and everything's over with."

Gracie Mae had one of my fingers clasped in her tight grip and her bottomless ink like eyes regarded me with amusement. I thought I heard her chuckle but it was probably just the wind.

"No," I whispered, smiling back at her. "I believe we're just getting started."